A Battleaxe and a Metal Arm 7:

Ill-Fated Voyage

Samuel Fleming

Thank you to my Beta Readers

and to my First Reader,

Mel.

Contents

"Many times I prayed for
death, and found my god and
savior silent."
—nameless

Previously...

After perishing at the wizard's tower, Helesys and Taunauk woke again in the dungeon. Shawn, the shadowy rogue, was nowhere to be found. The heroes were left with only his familiarity and the feeling that they would one day see him again.

The stone hallway led them to a mist-covered jungle. They walked carefully through this new realm, passing all manner of trees and birds, and strange carved totems that seemed to reach up through the mist and to the sky itself.

They were found by a tribe who worshipped the shadow-stepping giant, Logath. Of all the curiosities, bone jewelry and weapons were chief among them, and it didn't take the heroes long to find out the sinister reasons behind them. At the heart of the tribe was a roaring bonfire, upon which flesh and tributes were heaped—Terran meat. Those poor souls heaped upon the fire would no longer wander the realms, and would be trapped in a lingering death. Their flesh would become nourishment for the cannibal tribe.

The shamans held Taunauk with a spell, and Helesys held the village guards in turn. Just when it seemed no bluff or threat would save them, Taunauk's golden glow overcame the Shaman's holding spell. Rather than risk injury to the village, the cannibal shamans let them leave in peace.

But peace was short-lived. In their wandering, they came upon a bonefield of mindless, half-made creatures. It was there that one of the elven shaman set upon them with spells and by controlling the bone creatures. Helesys fought a battle of magic against her and the guards, while Taunauk fended off the bonemen. In the end, Helesys overwhelmed the shaman and stopped the battle with heated metal hand upon her throat.

Their wandering through the jungle, brought them to a clearing in the mist—the grotto of the serpent Irehyl, goddess of the lost. She presented a task to Helesys and Taunauk: To clear journey through the Nest of the Damned and down to the dwelling of the Apothecary—if they were to slay her, then the could extinguish the bonfire of the cannibal village and lift the mist that plagues the jungle.

The heroes set to task with newfound purpose and fought through the Damned, cackling half-made creatures, and eluded Logath. They descended the mines and confronted the Apothecary, but the witch and Logath ambushed them. Helesys was dragged through the wall of the cavern, to a space between to do battle with the giant, leaving Taunauk to fend for himself against the witch. Helesys made short work of the giant and found the Apothecary's weapons feeble against her glowing comrade.

The Apothecary had one final trick, turning into mist and planning to accost the heroes from every angle and render them slaves. Helesys turned her magic against her, amplifying her own spell and dispersing the Apothecary into millions of pieces.

They walked to the center of the witch's abode, and rested a piece of bone from the center of the great fire, collapsing it and ending the spell over the land.

But from the ends of the magic, the Apothecary returned, weakened, and quickly set upon by Irehyl—who tore her limb from limb. In the end, the heroes left the realm by Helesys magic for the first time, instead of death.

~ ~ ~

The Hallway

Helesys and Taunauk stepped through the portal from the Apothecary's cavern. The portal was opaque at first, hiding whatever lay on the other side. Whether this was some latent ward of the Apothecary or an unintended consequence of the magic, Helesys didn't know. She only knew that the path forward lay through it—that was the only reason either of them needed.

Her feet struck stone, and the elven weaver and human barbarian found themselves in the familiar hall. But this time they could see light at the end of the hall, whereas every other time their journey had started with a long walk.

There was something else too… a crunch beneath her boots. Helesys bent down and ran her elven hand over the stones and felt sparse sand.

Taunauk stowed Everfall and axe upon his back. He breathed deep. "Salt water." A moment later, Helesys smelled it too.

Helesys and Taunauk walked the endless hall with renewed vigor, both the lack of death and idea of escape fueling their steps. Sand crept into the hallway in earnest, covering the stone and finally growing deep enough for their boots to sink into. The smell of salt grew strong.

By the last hundreds of feet, the light was near blinding, the churn of waves echoed through the hall, and the pair had broken into a dash.

They ran out of the hallway and onto the dunes of a great beach. The sky was bright blue, almost blinding. The air was warm, and for a moment, Helesys thought she could feel the sun upon her face.. She relished in the most freedom she could remember. But it was a lie—the sky was bright, but there was no sun anywhere above them.

The beach stretched out to the horizon in either direction. Behind them lay the dungeon entrance, little more than a square hole in the sand. In front of them, an ocean of blue that glistened in the light. Waves taller than either of them churned and crashed upon the shore. In the distance to the right, lay a spire in the dunes.

In reality, the sun wasn't in the sky. It was just behind the horizon, doomed never to rise completely, save for those unknown, cosmic events.

She caught Taunauk's eye and found the outlander smiling softly, as if both the blue sky and the mirth of his comrade had cracked the stone of his facade, if only slightly. He was already slipping off his massive cloak and folding it beneath his arms.

"To task," he said, turning and striding across the sand.

Helesys followed, and the two walked in silence amongst the wind and the waves, toward the spire.

~

Though they walked upon the hard sand of the dunes, the walk began to wear on Helesys. She felt her face growing hot from the sunlight that reflected down on them and suspected that exposure was something most elves avoided. She kindled her wand-arm for endurance, striving to use as little as needed.

Beside her, Taunauk walked stoically. Helesys found herself envying the barbarian's endurance and his outlander complexion.

"We can stop to rest," Taunauk offered.

Helesys scoffed at his observance. "I can draw upon my wand for endurance if needed." It seemed most things did not escape his perception.

The outlander shrugged. "It was merely an offer. We should reach the tower by dark."

Helesys sighed. She would manage, but it brought back memories of her long walk to the infinite wall. At least this time, she was not alone. This time she had her comrade. Better that than enemies—of which the numbers were steadily growing.

She chuckled. "I fear we are making too many enemies."

"Are you speaking of the Apothecary?"

"Of her, the elven shaman, the green knight, Matron Mildé, Paraxnae, even Stizzai, Zhug's goblin captain… They are certainly more numerous than our allies."

"Enemies that we won't see again," Taunauk offered with a dismissive wave of his hand.

"Enemies that can't die," she countered. "And as their numbers grow, so does the chance that we will see one of them again."

"What do you suggest? Was it unwise to follow Irehyl and kill the Apothecary?"

Helesys turned a hard eye away from the waves and toward the dunes, to the infinite looking stretch of sand and to a dungeon she knew that lay across it—even if she could not see it.

She said, "I do not know whether we have been a tool in a personal vendetta rather than a noble one. Irehyl was careful not to mention her lover's bone at the heart of the Apothecary's fire. She might have used us for her own gain… Do you think gods lie as mortals do?"

Taunauk pondered before answering. "I think that absent gods do not lie as often as those that speak."

After a moment, Helesys shot him a look and found a smirk on his lips. "A gracious non-answer."

He shrugged. "It was you who asked a man of faint memory."

"Alright, point taken." The crashing waves punctuated the levity of the moment.

But Taunauk's face hardened. "I remember something. Wisdom I once heard that you might find useful: The plains of Endroggen are as beautiful as they are perilous. Great beasts, rival clans, even marauders prowl the grasslands. Some of the warriors are tasked with evening watch and morning watch. Both must stay awake during the night to keep watch over the village.

"No group of warriors alone shoulders the burden of night watch. We are told to be wary of straddling the line between shadow and light, lest we walk in darkness for too long and lose ourselves. Lest your eyes adapt and you become a creature of the night, no longer able to walk in the daytime. No longer able to live the waking hours with your fellows."

"You're speaking of Irehyl's request to kill the Apothecary. You worry that I will meddle in the realms and fall into darkness?"

Taunauk nodded, but kept his eyes on the dunes and the path in front of them.

Helesys pondered this, pushing her defensiveness away for the moment. Rarely was her comrade's wisdom unfounded.

"I will set my mind to task," she finally said. "Hopefully, purpose will guide me when I need to walk in darkness. When that fails, the words of a comrade shall stay me."

She looked to Taunauk and saw a fleeting smile at her reassurance. She added, "Odd that mantras and musing should return before other memories. But then, this is a strange place. An impossible place."

~ ~ ~

The Shoal

In spite of their trek, the distance to the castle seemed to grow. Now both Helesys and Taunauk had removed their cloaks and slung them over shoulder. Taunauk seemed to relish in the blue skies and sunlight, where her mundane arm already felt as if it was smoldering without the shield of her cloak.

The soft curves of the dunes and rhythmic waves seemed endless and unchanging—twice lulling Helesys into walking-dream—before they came upon a break in the pattern. The gulls were first, swarming like white, flying rats and drowning out the surf with their cries. Hundreds of them.

Then Taunauk pointed to the water. He noticed the subtle change in the waves first, for the difference was so slight that only a hunter's eyes could've spotted it: The waves were merely shorter, crashing shorter distances upon the sand, but once Helesys turned to it, she could not turn away. Her wand-arm hummed with anticipation and warning—as if it too hadn't noticed the danger lurking in the waves.

Seaweed rose to the surface in patches of green and brown. Then the water frothed and boiled, churning sand so that the water was completely clouded. Even the seaweed faded from view.

Then a vine shot up into the sky with the quickness of a serpent's strike and snared a gull. The bird was broken and twisted in the snare, and the vine pulled it down toward the sea with such slowness and deliberateness that it made Helesys's mouth fall agape—then she realized why: As the trapped gull floated down to the sea, its brethren swarmed it, nipping feathers and pieces of flesh from the still-living bird.

"They're eating it before it disappears," she whispered in spellbound shock.

Dozens of seaweed vines shot up now, grasping and snaring prey. Half of the arms recoiled violently—morsels for whatever creature hid beneath the waves. The rest of the arms languished in descent, luring still more of the flock. Once more the cycle repeated itself, the seaweed creature snaring nearly a third of the flock. Meanwhile, another third descended to the dunes to fight over feathered scraps.

"It is not natural," Taunauk said from beside her. "But one does what one must, be them Terran or beast."

Two gulls limped on the beach, both a bloody mess. Either freed somehow from the creature's grasp or fallen victim to the ravenous flock. Now that they were on the sand, they were no longer hounded from the sky. Instead, a swarm of mottled creatures ran from over the dunes—scarred and featherless gulls—who overran the injured birds and finished the feast.

Helesys thought back to the cannibals in the fog-laden jungle and the bonemen they controlled, her stomach turning with disgust. "Is there no mercy here?"

"Come, let us dwell on this no more." Taunauk led them up the empty dunes, away from the creature and both swarms. He pulled the cloak from over his shoulder, held it in both hands, and walked forward. He waved and snapped his cloak at the few gulls that turned toward them. Helesys grasped her cloak and fanned it likewise. In spite of their viciousness, none of the birds were desperate enough to commit to the larger, Terran prey.

~

Helesys and Taunauk walked the edge of the dunes and put the grisly scene behind them. The weaver looked back only once and saw the last of the gulls pulled beneath the surface. Soon, even the gulls that remained were quiet.

Sometime later, when the sun barely peeked over the horizon—at its pitiful crest—Helesys revisited her thoughts. Why was she so able to stomach the suffering of Terrans and the bonemen in the jungle realm, and why did the plight of the gulls wear upon her? What was the logic in that?

"What troubles you?" Taunauk asked.

Helesys smirked. "Your sense for inner turmoil is as strong as your sense for danger."

"It is written on your face as plainly as the sand." When she stayed silent, Taunauk added, "Give voice to it."

But the weaver shook her head under the blaring sky. "I still do not understand it myself."

"Where else would questions come from?"

Helesys shrugged. "I merely do not understand why I find some things repulsive and not others. I feel pity for the birds easier than for men and elves. It is easy to chalk it up to missing memory, and hope that in time I will regain understanding over those feelings. Perhaps remember how to control them."

Taunauk chuckled, a deep and resonating sound—one that took the elf by surprise. "If all Terrans controlled their feelings, then they would all fight as barbarians do."

"Is that the true nature of your blood magic, then? Merely controlling emotions."

"Yes," he scoffed. "As the true nature of combat is swinging a sword."

Helesys stopped on the dunes. "Then explain it to me. Do you remember?"

Taunauk paused and glanced at her sideways. Twice he looked across the dunes and back to her, as if he was reserved in sharing the secret of the Endroggen. And as they stood on the impossible shoreline, It was not lost on Helesys that they were perhaps as far as they could be from the barbarian homeland.

In spite of that, if Endroggen magic was something Helesys could wield, a weapon she could use, then she must know! "I have fought beside you, without reason and without qualm—"

"I know," Taunauk said calmly. He sighed deeply and looked out across the barren sands, and smiled as if he were looking over the fields of home. "Control is not all there is to Endroggen rage. It is not enough for clouds to build and darken the sky, nor roll over the landscape. It is not enough for the clouds to churn. The storm must break—be it in sweet rain or hellish torrent. Thunder can rumble or it can crack the sky. Lightning can flicker or it can split the earth.

"It is not enough to quell the storm. If it were, any wiseman would fight as I do. No. It is not enough to bottle the storm. It must be unleashed—and that takes more of an outlander."

Taunauk sighed again, frustrated with his explanation.

Helesys stepped forward, needing both to encourage her comrade and needing even more to understand. "Tell me. Where do your clouds come from?"

The outlander's eyes darkened. "From the plains of Endroggen. From a people I can scarcely remember and a family whose faces have been stolen from me. From a youth and a life forgotten, that haunt my dreams like a barren night sky. The laughter of comrades that has been taken from me. The theft of my world. A purpose that drives me, yet my tongue has forgotten it.

"These things dwell within me like blackened sky and fall with every crash of axe and—forgive me. Endroggen do not share these things… Not even with each other."

Taunauk's voice had risen with his explanation, and in those moments, Helesys thought she could see the very storm building within him—all gone in an instant, as if a candle had been snuffed and not even a wisp of smoke remained.

"Why don't you speak of them?" Helesys asked, undeterred.

"Rage is shared only with the enemy."

She nodded, then chuckled at her own question. "What of the other emotions?"

Taunauk glanced quizzically at her, as if snapped from his trance. "Laughter, passion, love, all are storm clouds to us. And all are in short supply here."

Helesys held up her hands in mock defensiveness. "You'll hear no quarrel from me. One day we'll find someone for you to share them with." She started to walk away, but turned to wave her comrade on. "I'm sorry to dwell on those things. Come Taunauk. Let us outpace the storm clouds."

The outlander nodded thoughtfully and then followed her across the dunes toward the castle on the horizon.

~ ~ ~

Castle in the Sand

What appeared at first to be a spire was a half-buried castle. Sand dunes came up to the windows of what should have been the second or third story. Of the windows, only twisted frames and splintered fragments of glass remained. Half a dozen spires rose up behind the most prominent one, struggling to stay above the sand.

The weaver and barbarian approached cautiously; Helesys did this, not because she suspected danger, but because it felt as if walking through a graveyard. Before they reached the embankment, Helesys stopped and stared.

Throughout their journeys, they had often heard of the smothering oppression of time, the withering that ground all to dust. Helesys felt as if she were staring down the proof of it; one of the omnipresent laws of the dungeon was writ small and intimate. Here was a dying thing, and some small part of Helesys wept for it.

"What is it?" Taunauk had turned and was regarding her with worry. Perhaps he thought it was a spell or something more nefarious than creeping dread.

Helesys shook her head. "It is nothing. Just poetry in the crumbling walls."

The barbarian nodded thoughtfully, as if he understood her meaning, or understood enough of it. Then he turned and continued up the sandy slope, as if expecting her to come along, anyway.

Helesys knew then that there were things here which she could not reconcile: She could not face realm after realm and certain, uncountable deaths, not while staring at a crumbling castle, a trapped god, or a forgotten civilization. She could do nothing, except continue forward—lest she be ground to dust and buried like all the rest.

They climbed the sand and up through a broken window, which was nearly two stories tall itself. The inside was covered in sand, turning what might've been a towering five story grand hall into one merely a story or two high, and where the rafters were close enough to touch but otherwise unbroken. Boxes, blankets and bottles littered the sand. At first glance, the arrangement looked haphazard—but blankets were piled near boxes and bottles were half-filled with water and positioned away from the scant rays of light that filtered through the cracks in the roof. A single shield hung from the rafters on the left wall like a trophy. It's face was silver, plain and polished to a high sheen so that it gleamed, even in the faint light. Then Taunauk pointed to the far wall, to another dune entrance and tracks in the sand.

"Do you think we spooked them?" Helesys asked.

Taunauk looked quickly over the scene again, hands hanging empty. "Perhaps. Or they merely ventured from their dwelling. No weapons…"

Helesys looked again at the polished shield. "That does not look used either. Nor do I feel any warning from my wand-arm."

Without saying further, Taunauk walked across the room, stepping carefully around the blankets—for posterity, rather than trying to hide his tracks—and led Helesys over the inhabitants' tracks.

They walked up to the opposite exit to the slope of the castle and paused just outside the wall. Tracks led off around the outside of the castle. At the bottom of the slope were two surprised and haggard human men, each cradling water jugs. Their hair and beards were long, twisted, and unkempt. Their clothes looked like rags stitched together, and where skin showed, both men were as tan as boiled leather.

Taunauk stepped aside from the entrance, then held a hand up in greeting. "We are passersthrough."

Helesys stepped to the other side, following Taunauk's gesture. When the men didn't move, she said, "We would have words and shade, if you would share it."

The elder of the two men, with twists of white in his beard, nodded slowly. "Those we have." Then the two men led Helesys and Taunauk back into the castle hovel.

~

Inside, the two men sat their jugs down on the sand. The slosh from inside the containers caused Helesys's stomach to growl, which she promptly silenced with a burn of her wand-arm.

The wiry elder's name was Jarek. The younger and quieter of the two was Blom. Though he didn't speak in greeting, Blom grabbed two blankets; one each for Helesys and

Taunauk to sit on. He handed one to Taunauk, and moved to unfurl Helesys's blanket for her, but the weaver grasped it from the air.

"That's alright," she said. "I will do it myself."

Blom released it and cast his eyes downward before taking his seat on a blanket near Jarek. The two men sat cross-legged and with a relaxed ease, as if they'd both washed ashore and ended up precisely where they meant to be. Of the two men, only Jarek met their eyes. Glom looked aimlessly at the sand between them, though he appeared to be listening.

"So, you survived the dunes," Jarek said while Helesys and Taunauk unfurled their blankets. "That is no easy feat. But then you do not look like most who stumble upon the beach."

"Do many make it this far?" Helesys asked.

"Not this far."

Blom whispered, "Many dangers on the shore."

Jarek nodded and leaned forward to hand a clay jug to Helesys and another to Taunauk. "It is tea. Please drink. We distil seawater and use the grasses just over the dune. It is bitter, but it is better than nothing."

Taunauk sat on the blanket and pulled off his boots to reveal thin socks. He turned the boots over and shook out a pile of sand. "It's as bad as mist." He looked to Jarek and asked, "Have you no food? No fish?" before putting his boots back on.

The white-bearded Jarek sighed. "The dead do not stay here and so it is damned hard to eat your fill. Kill a fish and it is dead before you can cook it. Fell a tree for firewood and in the morning it is gone. Even the grasses do not stay."

Helesys drank the tea and wiped drippings from her lips—she saw now why the elder looked so apologetic over the bitter drink. "The grasses stay long enough to make tea."

"Only just," he replied. "For all I know, it is no more than remnants of salt from the sea."

Helesys slung her pack from her shoulders and reached in. She pulled a ration out and handed it to Jarek, watching to see his reaction.

Jarek's eyes went wide and he smelled at the half-wrapped jerky. Then he shook his head and handed it to Glom, who held it as if it was a precious jewel.

"There's more," the weaver said. "We can spare a few rations."

"No, thank you," Jarek said firmly. He glanced sideways at his younger companion as Glom began to unwrap the jerky and nibble at the edges. Jarek shrugged and pointed to Glom. "Perhaps another ration for *him*. It's not good for the soul to taste something so nice, not when we're used to surviving on tea, half-eaten gulls."

"What of eggs?" Taunauk asked suddenly.

"They don't last. The gulls eat them within minutes."

Glom muttered between bites, "I haven't had an egg in months." His arms were flexed, as if it was taking willpower to eat the jerky as slowly as he was.

Helesys eyed Jarek. "Are your objections moral or religious, then?"

Jarek shook his head. "It's taken long to forget the pangs of hunger. A few minutes to savor it would start it anew. I will not suffer hunger like that again."

Glom paused eating just long enough to speak. "It's the same as surfing."

"What's that?" Jarek asked. "What are you on about?"

The younger man spoke whilst holding the meat inches from his face. "We surf. Then we wait two days to do it again."

"Surf?" Taunauk grumbled, finally taking the stopper out to drink from the jug. "What does that mean?" He drank in two quick, great gulps, then set the half-empty jug back down.

Jarek pointed to the silver shield, the lone relic hanging from the rafters. "He speaks of our tradition. Every third morning, we take the Shield of Vitrum down to the waves and utter the magic words. Then one climbs atop the board and swims out past the breaking waves, turns round and rides atop the surging waves back to the shore." Jarek motioned his hand curving back and forth across the front of a wave.

Helesys and Taunauk exchanged a glance of confusion.

The barbarian shrugged. "That is one way to spend eternity."

Helesys looked upon the weary men in disbelief. They'd been living off grass tea and scavenging meat. "How… How long have you been doing this?"

"Some twenty years," Jarek said. "But we stopped keeping track long ago, back when there were more of us and when the castle wasn't full of sand. We are the last two. All others have wandered farther down the shore."

Glom added, "or drowned themselves."

Two more who haven't the strength to wander, she thought. Helesys turned from the men, not from disgust but from pity, and her eyes fell upon the hanging shield. Fading light trickled in from holes in the roof and glinted off its surface.

The things men hold on to.

"Stay here," Jarek said. "Stay the night. You can see for yourself. Perhaps then you will understand."

~

Taunauk resigned himself to sleeping in the corner of the sandy hovel for the rest of the afternoon so that he could take first evening watch. He did this in spite of Jarek's reassurances that the night was just as safe as the day—at least around the castle.

The sun was disappearing and turning the color of coals in the sky. The beauty of sunrise and sunset was writ short on the sky. The waves slowed from a crash to a tumble, no longer spurred on by the wind.

Glom went foraging for more grasses to make the evening's ration of tea. Helesys found herself wandering the dunes and Jarek walking beside her. He was content to answer any and all of her questions, though he asked none in return. It seemed to Helesys that the reasoning was similar to why he declined their rations—that he would long for realms of which he wouldn't taste again.

"And you're sure it's safe here? Even along the shore?" Helesys asked as he led them down to the lapping waves. She trusted Jarek—and her wand-arm offered no warning—but she had no desire to wind up like the poor gulls they had seen earlier that day.

Jarek nodded. "Yes. The castle's magic extends across this stretch of beach. Don't ask me how far or for how long it extends, for it's magic was here long before Glom or I or anyone we knew. But no one has perished and been sent wandering while on this stretch of beach."

"I shall trust you," the weaver said idly. She looked out across the waves and tried to picture the two men *surfing*, and smiled at the thought. "It seems ridiculous. Tell me, how does one ride the waves on a metal shield?"

"With great skill," he replied in jest. "Like the castle, there is magic in the Shield of Vitrum. The magic words were passed down from our predecessors who had only the vaguest inkling of their original use. They claimed the shield is the embodiment of wisdom and that uttering the magic words make the shield and the bearer lighter by releasing the worldly weights of emotion."

"What does it feel like when you ride the waves?" Helesys asked, wanting to coax more out of him.

"It… It guides the bearer as we ride the waves…" Jarek trailed before adding, "Forgive me. It's a strange thing to understand the magic when I'm surfing. Yet I cannot communicate it to you now. It's as if the shield speaks in flashes of insight and that they disappear afterward. Something *felt* and not heard."

Helesys nodded along as they strode in the sand. She held out her metal arm and sunlight glinted off it as she turned her hand over. "My gauntlet speaks in a similar fashion. Warning or insight comes without being spoken aloud. So I understand your meaning. Yet you speak of magic being felt when you leave worldly emotions behind. Feeling the magic, yet not feeling emotion, is a *difficult* truth."

Jarek shrugged. "It's a truth for surfing, not for life. Emotions are worldly and perhaps wisdom is not?"

"You said that emotions can be a burden… What would you say of barbarian rage? Taunauk calls it blood magic—the bottling of emotions to be unleashed later upon an enemy."

Jarek thought on this a moment. "Most interesting. Most warriors claim to want a clear mind during battle. A mind free of emotion so that training can carry them through. But clearly they are a boon when tempered…"

Their pace slowed to a stop on the sand and Helesys found her gaze drifting off across the ocean.

When Helesys could not bear the silence any longer, she asked, "Why do you stay here on this stretch of beach? Is it merely the safety of the castle?"

"I suppose safety is an anchor, but there's more than just that." He turned to the waves now and gestured with his hands as he spoke. "Do you see how the waves swell differently along the stretch. Now look at the breaks; those are different as well. They are different at morning, midday and evening. One can spend a lifetime getting to learn the shifting terrain of the sand and the waves—and that is just here on this single solitary stretch!

"Imagine a sparring partner," Jarek said. "Imagine fighting them and only them all your life. Would they ever become predictable?"

Helesys shook her head. "I think not. They would learn as I learn."

"They would change as you did. It is the same here. No two waves are the same, just as no two fights would be. Glom and I have spoken of it—the few times he does speak—we will stay here until the castle sinks into the sand and its magic is lost along with it. Leaving would be a tragedy." Jarek turned to her and said, "To your earlier question about barbarian rage, it seems like the bottling of emotions is only a boon because it is tempered with wisdom. Knowing precisely when and how to unleash it."

"What if one could separate the two completely?" Helesys asked.

"We all have emotion and wisdom within us. Terrans by our very nature have both. Separating them would lead to impotence or turmoil."

~

As the sun set, Helesys took Taunauk's place in the sand hovel. The barbarian bid them good evening before taking his watch. Jarek and Glom lay down to sleep on their own blankets and were asleep nearly as soon as their heads hit the sand.

She dreamed of white sands and white sky, a flash of some incomprehensible plane or some mirrored version of their own. It was over as quickly as it began.

She woke to Taunauk's footsteps in the sand as he entered the castle hovel.

Helesys rose, drank tea, and moved to take her watch shift.

"It's as peaceful as they say," Taunauk whispered as she passed. "See you in the morn."

Helesys nodded and passed beside him, out into the moonlit beach. The sight made her pause. Of all the things, she thought, it is strange that a moon should be lost as well. But past the moon were the stars, and if it were trapped, then weren't the stars trapped too?

Helesys stood on the edge of the beach as if the water were a cliff's edge and passed more time there in silent contemplation that she would later admit.

Jarek and Glom came out at the first light of Dawn. Jarek carried a jug of tea and Glom carried the Shield of Vitrum on top of his head. Morning sun glinted off the face of it. Taunauk followed them, carrying Helesys's pack.

The trio stopped and stood beside her, just on the edge of the lapping waves.

Jarek set the jug down. "My family had a blessing they offered to passersthrough. One about the returning of the sun each day and the moon each night, how there is truly no such thing as *goodbye*. For a while, I said similar things here, even changing it to reflect the returning of the waves. They come, they go back out, and return again. Here we see scarce few return, but you… I fear that we may see you again. I fear that you will not be sated or beaten easily. So instead, I offer you a blessing of peace: That you shall find it in your travels. That one day you will not be strangers in a strange land, but that you would find home or make it somewhere."

The old surfer offered his hand, and shook with Helesys and then Taunauk. Glom merely nodded.

Then the two men walked ankle deep into the waves. Jarek stooped down, cupped seawater and sprinkled it over the Shield of Vitrum. Then he and Glom spoke the magic words so that his voice echoed over the waves. As he did, Helesys wand-arm translated and she whispered the prayer in the common tongue to Taunauk.

"Libera me ab his manicis orbis terrarum." Deliver me from the shackles of the world…

"Et ego potest tangere caelum." So that I can touch the heavens…

"Immensae, informem, intempus." Boundless, formless, timeless…

"immortalitatis in fluctus." Immortality in the waves.

Jarek and Glom whispered the final words and then Jarek walked out into the waves with the Shield of Vitrum.

Helesys found herself dwelling on the last line of the magic words, because they were not part of the spell. They were merely words—merely a blessing—added on by some surfer before Jarek and Glom.

When he was waist deep in the sea, he laid on the back of the shield and began to paddle out over the waves. And when he was at the minor swells, the very beginnings of the ripples, he turned round and floated on the shield.

Moments dragged on in the rising sun and though they did not wonder aloud, twice Glom insisted quietly that they wait. All the while, Jarek lay prone on the shield and waited.

At some perfect moment, seemingly indifferent from the rest, Jarek paddled furiously. At first, Helesys thought he was trying to chase a wave, then realized he was trying to stay just in front of one—the shield and the surfer were spurred on by the wave. And when the shield drew a wake off its sides, Jarek leapt to his feet. Half-crouched, he balanced on the shield and turned it so he slipped parallel to the wave—somewhere moving all the quicker as he did.

Helesys watched with a growing smile on her face as Jarek turned round in front of the wave and slipped across its front in the opposite direction. He snaked back and forth, staying just ahead of the growing wave, until it was nearly on the shore and it began to crest and roll overhead.

Jarek disappeared behind the face of the wave and reappeared several moments later—having outrun the crashing water. He leapt off the shield and carried it across the surf toward them. He offered it to Glom and then the younger man waded out into the waves.

Helesys and Taunauk watched thrice more before they finally left the surfers to the glory of the third day. Both elf and outlander had smiles across their faces at having witnessed some moments of peace in their journey.

And long after they had left, Helesys whispered a blessing for the surfers. "*Ut immortalitatis invenis.*"

May you find immortality.

~ ~ ~

The Ill–Fated Voyage

The weaver and the barbarian walked the endless shore for another solemn day before they found other signs of life. In the distance, they saw the mast of a ship and as they approached, they saw the great body of it run aground on the shore. People milled about—from that distance, no bigger than ants.

It was only when the heroes approached that they saw the true scale of the scene. The ship was a double mast, some one hundred and fifty feet long. Its back half was laden in the sand and waves lapped at the front. Crew milled all around, their clothes coated in sweat and sand. Some rolled barrels up the main ramp. Others ran rigging through the masts or hung fresh planks on the side of the ship and painted lacquer over the fresh planks. In all, Helesys counted some fifty men and women among the crew—several children too, who ran small bags of supplies to the craftsmen.

And as Helesys and Taunauk approached, whispers spread amongst the crew, though the work did not stop.

A wiry man approached them. He wore a red vest and hair wrap with a set of crisscrossing gold bars woven into both.

Braided hair hung past his shoulders, with dark red twine woven in. His hands were smeared with the dark lacquer, which smelled deeply of pine and earth.

He smiled with sun-beaten warmth. "*Saludecae.* All are welcome here if they are willing to work… and you both look like you can pull your weight. I am Captain Besting. Jimdonawie Besting. Do you have any skills? Rigging, carpentry, fishing?"

Both Helesys and Taunauk exchanged glances and then shook their heads. Helesys said, "We are strong and able to learn."

The Captain looked them over with a curious eye, lingering for just a moment on her metal arm. "Strength is always needed. Unfortunately, weapons are needed too, along with those that wield them." He nodded. "Welcome aboard the ship, *Malorienta.*"

Helesys asked, "Where are you sailing?"

Besting raised an eyebrow. "*Away.* Past the reef and out to the farthest reaches—anywhere but here. Is that satisfactory?"

Before Helesys could agree, a familiar shout came from the deck of the ship. "Gods, aren't you a sight for landlocked eyes!"

All three turned their gaze upward and saw Shawn standing on the railing of the *Malorienta.* He pulled a tunic down over a tattoo-covered torso and black wrappings around his arms. The rogue fell gracefully from the railing, somersaulted, and landed on the sand with an otherworldly grace, then sauntered up to them with open arms.

Besting asked, "You've met them before?"

Shawn nodded and stopped beside the Captain. "I can personally vouch for them, both their tenacity and their skillful violence." The rogue flashed a playful smile.

"And their character?"

"Of course, that too," Shawn added quickly.

This was the first time Helesys had seen the rogue without his hood pulled overhead, and so the first time she had seen his face clearly. His features were sharp and deeply tan from his time in the sun. His eyes were the same piercing blue… But the most striking detail was that his ears did not match. The right ear was pointed like an elf's, but the left ear looked cropped. After another glance, Helesys realized that it did not look scarred, but natural—as if Shawn was born with both an elven ear and a human ear.

Shawn noticed her gaze. "What should they start with, Captain?"

Besting stroked his beard in thought. "There's not much work left to be done. Nothing that they could learn in two days. For now, load supplies. Underway, we'll find another use for you." Besting nodded and walked off, leaving the three heroes beside themselves with faint smiles.

It was Taunauk who broke the silence first with outstretched hand. "It is good to see you again."

Helesys offered her elven hand as well, which Shawn shook a moment later.

"Come on," Shawn said. "Reunions and tales can wait until we're underway. Maybe then you can tell me your secret."

"Secret?" Helesys asked.

"For getting here when the damned work is almost done! Some of us have been here for weeks."

~

Helesys and Taunauk spent the rest of the evening loading barrels filled with fresh water and grasses. Meanwhile, Shawn ran rigging and threaded the sails with easy grace, and the fleeting question of his origins returned to her. For now, the question was dismissed as quickly as the rogue climbed the mast, and Helesys resolved to ask him if more of his memories had returned in their time apart.

It felt good to work. The steady monotony of earnest labor was something so different from the perils of combat. She welcomed the sensations, rather than using her wand-arm to stave off the sweat and dull burn in the muscles of her legs, arms, and back. They quieted her mind and kept it from wandering too far from task.

The rest of the crew worked in similar fashion, in quiet solidarity. Helesys had only seen a gathering of commoners once before, in the Deacon's village in the Wode. She thought back to that humble place, one ruled by fear and awe… One in which Helesys had experienced a turmoil of emotions. One at first attributed to the villagers living under such a creature, but she came to realize her conflicting emotions stemmed from the Deacon, himself—that a creature of his terrible powers should give up wandering, cease trying to escape, and resign themselves to lordship in this place. It was a pattern repeated again and again in the dungeon by trapped warriors and bottled gods. All powerless.

There was still an uneasiness that permeated the crew, but seen only fleetingly. Sometimes a crew member would pause in their work and stare out into the distance, their attention falling inward to some terrible memory or dreadful thought. A few of the men paused to stare out over the sea with the same paralyzing dread. But it seemed as if working together in shared hope spared them from the larger plight.

Then there were the times the crew's eyes fell upon Helesys or Taunauk. It might have been curiosity, for Helesys and

Taunauk did not look like the others. There were no other Endroggen, save for Taunauk, and even the few elves were not of Helesys's stature or strength. Only some of the crew looked like warriors—those that carried swords on their hips or bows on their backs. Or perhaps it was simply their strength. Taunauk carried two barrels on his shoulders as easily as pairs carried one. Only Helesys and the stronger men carried a single barrel by themselves. Either way, Helesys felt akin to the Deacon in those moments—that the crew looked upon her and Taunauk with not just wonder, but expectation.

Shawn seemed spared the brunt of the crew's curiosity, but if he'd been here as long as he alluded to, then perhaps curiosity had run its course.

As the sun set, the work slowed to a stop. There were no more barrels to be brought. No more rigging or lacquer needed. A stew was prepared from the bitter grasses, nuts, berries, and squash from far over the dunes. And when the aroma wafted over the deck and across the sand, Captain Besting called the crew aboard.

They gathered, shoulder to shoulder, on the deck, weary and hopeful. He stood on the top deck and lay his hands on the railing. Helesys, Taunauk, and Shawn stood at the back of the crowd and listened with their brethren.

"The days have been long with work and sweat, and they will be longer still. Tonight marks our last night ashore. Tomorrow we shall set out across the sea toward whatever new fate lies across the waves. Tomorrow, when we straddle the horizon, when there is nothing but blue skies and blue sea, wind and salt and sun… Then you will know a taste of freedom. Tonight, eat, rest, and be merry."

Then Captain Besting nodded solemnly, dismissing the gathering. Even as the crew milled about and sought food below decks, the captain stayed on the top deck. He leaned on the railing and watched over them as they went.

"He's got a way with words," Shawn said from beside them. Of all the crew, the three of them hadn't moved. "Every few days, he does a speech like that."

The three waited until most of the crew had gone and some had returned before they too went below decks.

~

Helesys ducked under most of the overhangs as they descended down the stairwell before they came to the inner deck. The main sections of deck were open with sleeping hammocks hung all throughout for the crew and sparsely lit with arcane torches, both smokeless and cold-flamed. Some crew had taken their bowls and ate either on the floor or in their hammock. Captain Besting seemed to be walking between groups, perhaps offering words of encouragement.

Shawn led them farther toward the rear of the ship. There was the galley and the scent of bitter spices.

The rogue pointed down the adjacent stairwell. "That leads to the cargo hold and the bottom of the hull."

"You alluded earlier that you've been here long." Helesys said. She felt along the low ceiling with her mundane hand to know when to duck.

Shawn counted on one hand, twice through. "More than a week, less than two."

Helesys said, "Time doesn't make sense here. We have only been in the realm for two days. One other realm before that for a single day."

Taunauk grumbled, "Little makes sense here."

Shawn stepped into the galley and aside so that Helesys and Taunauk could enter. Here the ceiling raised up so that Helesys could stand up, though Taunauk bowed his head. The cook, a squat elf with a shaved head and dirty apron, pointed them toward bowls and the line. The three filed in at the back of the soup line, the smell of salt and sweat mixing with the soup in the tight confines. They filed through silently, and Shawn led them back up the stairs to the main deck.

"Might as well eat in the fresh air," Shawn said. He led them toward the bow, which faced out over the starlit waves.

Helesys glanced over the empty bow, then over the rest of the ship. The only other groups that ate on the main deck were back toward the torchlit stairwell. "Did you mean to bring us somewhere secluded?"

The rogue shrugged and sat cross-legged on the deck. "Solitude is hard to come by on a ship, even one still on the land."

Taunauk sat in similar fashion, while Helesys chose to lean against the short wall that surrounded the edge of the ship.

Shawn took a sip from his bowl. "Personally, I can take or leave the people. I was hoping to be reborn somewhere dryer this time." He gestured behind him. "The thought of sailing out there doesn't really appeal to me."

"Nor I," Taunauk grumbled from behind his bowl.

Helesys eyed him. "Don't tell me—you were in the realm of the fishmen?"

"Aye. Slippery bastards. I'm just happy to be above ground and to see the sky and the moon."

The weaver smiled and recounted their journey through the mist-laden jungle, the cannibal tribe, the bonemen and the Damned. Finally, she told him of the Apothecary and Logath the giant, and how she was able to open a seam between the realms—to cross through to another plane without needing to die.

"Now *that* is a useful skill," Shawn replied.

Helesys shook her head. "I fear it is limited in its usefulness. That was the first realm I've felt where the seams were weak enough to open them. Besides, we cannot just walk into the Wolf King's throne room. We are not prepared."

Shawn said, "Aye. Not after seeing what the Wolf-King did to Amadeus in his own sanctum."

Taunauk slurped the rest of his soup and set it on the deck. "Walking between realms will not help us. We need to scour the realms for weapons and magic."

The three shared a look of agreement, which was interrupted by bootsteps on the deck. Captain Besting wandered over and sat with them. Helesys cast her gaze downward at the intrusion, reminding herself that they were guests on his ship.

"I hope the gruel is satisfactory," Besting said with a grin. "Our cook has grown quite good at preparing it." The three answered with tentative slurps before he continued. "I have a task for you—one that comes before all others. This is a dangerous realm. Do not let this peaceful beach fool you. I don't know what we'll find once we get past the breakers, but I imagine we will need protection."

Besting's voice wavered—something so faint, Helesys nearly missed it. He was going to ask for their protection, yet their captain was obviously not practiced in *asking* for such things.

"Most of my crew are honest and hardworking, but they are not fighting men. I can count the Terrans good with a blade on a single hand—"

Taunauk lowered his bowl and all eyes fell upon him. "Say no more. All Terrans have their merits and we will earn our keep. Ancestors willing, we will all live long enough to learn other necessary tasks—to become a hammer and not just an axe."

Helesys half-smiled at the wisdom of her comrade. His words were firm and reassuring, sparing the captain from lowering himself, yet they brought to mind rending a suffering animal. It was a grisly, utilitarian image. One befitting an outlander.

Besting nodded in agreement, a fleeting smile passing across his face, before turning to other topics. "Shawn, something you said earlier intrigued me. You said you know these two? That you've crossed paths before."

The rogue nodded along, eyeing the captain suspiciously.

"But not reborn together?"

"No."

Besting eyed all of them in turn. "Do you understand that this is a rare detail? There is no such thing as coincidence in this world."

Helesys said, "We assume that we knew each other in our lives before, but those memories are still lost to us."

"Rare," Shawn muttered. "Just how rare?"

Captain Besting waved a dismissive hand. "I've never heard the likes of it before. Everyone I've heard of is either reborn together or, more likely, never see each other again."

"What does it mean?" Taunauk asked.

The Captain shrugged and then stood. "I don't know. I just know that it's rare, and I wanted to hear it for myself before rumors spread through the crew." Besting nodded and then walked off to join the rest, leaving them in silence.

When they were alone again, Helesys asked, "Did you tell them anything else about us? Or that we can bring things back?"

Shawn shook his head. "No. I make it a point to only share the pertinent details."

She eyed his single cropped ear, then pointed to it. "What about that, then?"

The rogue ran a hand over the human-like ear. "Oh that? I'm not exactly sure." He smirked. "Really, I'm not. Might have been a mark for my thieving ways."

"It doesn't look scarred," Helesys added. "Maybe your parents were human and elven."

Shawn shrugged. "At the moment, your guess is as good as mine."

"Would you share it with us?" she asked. "If you remembered."

"With you and with you," Shawn said, gesturing to Helesys and then Taunauk. "We're in a different boat, as it were, then these poor souls."

Taunauk picked up his bowl and stood. "Of that, we can agree." Then he turned to walk away.

"Going back for seconds?" Shawn called.

"Yes."

~ ~ ~

The Reef

They slept on the crew deck, taking hammocks toward the bow of the ship. Helesys managed to sleep, in spite of the sequential snoring of the crew throughout the hold.

At dawn, the *Malorienta* was unceremoniously pushed from the shore by a dozen of the men, including Helesys and Taunauk. They waded out, pushing her through the short, breaking waves. Once the ship was floating and ready to sail properly, they climbed a set of spare rigging and rejoined the rest of the crew on deck.

Captain Besting was at the helm and calling orders. Above, Shawn and other runners let down the mainsails, and the deckhands turned the mast at an angle and the *Malorienta* lumbered forward. Helesys's stomach lurched with the ship and she grasped the side railing during those tumultuous first minutes through the breakers.

In spite of her unease, it was a sight to behold to see so many working in unison. It hadn't occurred to her that the ship would have so many necessary roles to fill. The image of her gauntlet came to mind, with dozens or hundreds or moving pieces, all aligning in necessary order to channel its power. The

ship was much the same; the sails had to be turned and unfurled to varying degrees so as to catch the wind efficiently—
too much or too little wind, both presenting problems.
Though the weaver didn't know the exact workings of her
gauntlet, she knew enough to appreciate its inner mechanisms,
as she appreciated the scurrying movement of the crew of the
Malorienta.

Taunauk was beside her, grasping the railing with both
hands. Knuckles white, face tense. His eyes flitted between the
surf, the railing, and the horizon.

"Have you been on a ship before?" Helesys asked.

"Once. The memory is fleeting and powerful, and it is cruel
that I could not recall it until now."

"It wasn't a good voyage?"

"It was serviceable." Beads of sweat grew on Taunauk's
brow. "I prefer the ground beneath my feet. If I were meant
for the sea, I would have been born with a fish tail." The barbarian managed a smile amidst his turmoil.

Helesys turned her attention back to the shallow sea, wait-
ing and hoping for her own memory to return. But as the
moment dragged on and the *Malorienta* cut toward the dark
blue ocean, the weaver was left with only a feeling of familiarity. Helesys knew that she had been on ships before and felt
that they were an overall pleasant experience, but that was all.
Hope faded and was replaced with a curse for the dungeon.
Damn whatever gods may be.

From the helm, Captain Besting called out over the wind
and waves, "We're approaching the reef. Be ready!"

The shallows were a crystal blue with a smattering of white,
but in the distance, Helesys saw a line of gray, like a stain upon
the sea. It stretched out across the shallows all the way to either
horizon. From where she stood, there seemed no way around.

They would need to go over the reef… Helesys set her gaze upon the gray line in the water and resolved to trust the captain.

Meanwhile, her wand-arm began to hum, something that had started so faintly it was indiscernible from the slosh of the waves. She let go of the railing with her metal arm and then felt the alarm clearly. It built as they approached the reef, the quiet hum becoming a discerning rattle.

"Something comes," Helesys said, loud enough for Taunauk to hear. Then the gray water began to boil—a frothing section to the left and more than twice the size of the *Malorienta*. "At arms," she yelled back to the crew and pointed toward the waves. Captain Besting echoed her call.

Besting steered the *Malorienta* to the right, and for a moment it looked like they might pass by the disturbance without trouble. Then the boiling water swelled and pushed upward, and a huge rocky mass rose up out of the water.

"Hold on tight!" Shawn yelled from the tops of the rigging. The displaced waves crashed against the hull and the *Malorienta* lurched hard to the right. Several crew were thrown across the deck, but thankfully none from the rigging above.

The ship rocked in the new waves and as they came round the rocky mass, Helesys saw it in earnest. The back of the beast was the color of stone, but covered in all manner of electric-bright colors of coral and fish trapped and flopping between. Its face was a twisted mass of eyes, mandibles and whiskers. At the base, a dozen equally dark legs were visible, and to the side, an enormous pincher claw rose up out of the water, nearly as big as the body of the crab and nearly as big as the *Malorienta*, itself. The rising claw sent another series of lurching waves toward the ship and over the bow. The thick shell of the beast creaked and groaned as the pincher snapped in anticipation of its prey.

But even with the crab's monstrous weapon revealed, Helesys's wand-arm grew steadily louder with warning.

Blobs of water congealed on the upper shell of the beast and then started to pulse and swirl. In the half-dozen spots, waterspouts grew like tendrils. They lengthened and reached nearly all the way to the ship. Helesys thought of the injured water elemental back in the flooded temple and its swirling body.

Even though the giant crab was half-submerged, its legs thundered under the waves with terrible quickness. In moments, it would be upon them.

Screams broke out across the ship. The few children and older Terrans had the sense to run for the stairs and safety of the interior of the ship, but even that would not matter if the creature made it to them.

Helesys churned power and purple lightning crackled across her metal fingers. Fear gave way to thrill, and she greeted the bottled violence like an old friend. She leveled her gauntlet and blasted directly at the creature's face; the recoil sending her back two paces on the deck.

The arcane blast slammed into the giant crab, just above the creature's face. The impact sent chunks of rock and shell flying across the water and the creature let out a high-pitched, crackling roar. But its steps paused only a moment before the creature ducked beneath the waves and continued toward them.

Out of the corner of her vision, Helesys saw the tendrils of water reach the deck and were answered by a barbarian's roar. Taunauk met the swirling arms with a wild flurry of his axe. With each slash, the end of the tendril splashed harmlessly on the deck, as if it were flesh that had been severed. But still, the tendrils came. Each time they were cut, they grew back moments later.

A trailing cloth fell from the rigging—Shawn, with twin daggers in hand. He hit the deck and sprinted from end to end, meeting tendrils that Taunauk's axe did not reach. Two other sailors had drawn blades and were protecting Captain Besting while he steered the *Malorienta* away.

All the while, Helesys was churning power again—this time calling upon the Ring of Winter and feeling the swirls of cold joining the acne power bottled inside her gauntlet. She braced herself, and let loose a barrage of power which streaked across the waves. Purple and white exploded against the shell, sending rock and coral flying. Two blasts struck low on the waves, freezing chunks of seawater. Still. the crab lumbered toward them.

In the chaos of the moment, the *Malorienta* was changing course—their path arching ever more to the right—as the notion of sailing past the beast turning into *outrunning it*. As the ship turned, the tendrils could no longer reach the side, but could reach Captain Besting. Helesys turned and ran toward the rear of the ship, in time to see Taunauk and Shawn leaping up to the Captain's deck to follow the tendrils of water.

A moment later, Taunauk and Shawn were a blur of violence on the back deck. The two sailors that had so valiantly protected the captain, now huddled close by, their weapons nearly rendered moot by the two veteran warriors. The massive arcs of Taunauk's axe reached nearly from post to post, and Shawn struck so fast that he seemed like a streak of lightning. Each strike momentarily severed the magic of the water tendrils, but each regrew in mere moments.

But by the time Helesys reached the deck, the crab was almost upon them, the massive pincher claw crashing within mere feet of the ship, each swing causing the ship to lurch—and if it turned too much and lost speed, then they were doomed.

Helesys reached deep into her well of power, hoping that there was some way to slow or completely hold the monster. Either spell worked with deadly efficiency against enemies her own size, but against larger creatures it was like trying to hold back a ruptured dam—an impossible task. Even summoning the limits of her power for an arcane blast might not stay the creature.

The Ring of Winter pulsed expectantly on her finger, and Helesys thought of the frozen chunks of water left in the wake of the cold blasts.

Helesys ran past her comrades, slipping under and around their bodies and blades, and ducked under the tendrils, and leaned against the back railing. She churned power, compounding the bottled energy and called upon the Ring of Winter. She held tight to the railing, aimed just in front of the beast, and let go of her wand-arm.

A mix of frost and purple exploded from her gauntlet, and sent her lurching backward and nearly off her feet. The water erupted, sending salty spray across the deck and causing the ship to lurch as if it were climbing uphill. Then the color seeped out of the sea, flashing from blue to white. There was a deep, horrid crack and a bellowing shriek from the giant crab. The swirls and boils of the sea between the ship and the monster froze solid, and the crab lurched to a halt.

Though the *Malorienta* lurched forward and backward, it thankfully continued on, the ice not having stopped it.

Helesys, Taunauk, Shawn, and the other sailors on the top deck watched with bated breath as the beast was halted by the ice. Ice clung to the creature's body, frost to its upper shell. It roared again, impotent against the icy confines.

No more than moments later, the crab swung its massive claw down. The strike was so loud it sounded like thunder and the ice splintered under the blow. Two strikes later and the ice was broken and floating away.

But the *Malorienta* was half-a-dozen ship lengths away and the giant crab turned back toward the reef.

The two sailors dropped their swords and erupted into whoops and cheers. Taunauk and Shawn let their blades relax. Helesys leaned heavy against the railing.

"What in the blazes was that?" Shawn asked. He holstered his left blade and raised the hand to shield his eyes from the glinting sun.

Silence fell upon the deck.

"An impossible question," Taunauk said quietly. "All manner of beast and being are trapped here."

"Don't go relaxing just yet," Captain Besting said. "I fear there will be more perils on this journey."

"Aye," Shawn said, before flipping his right knife and tucking it away in his invisible pouch. "Of that, we can be sure."

Besting turned to the two sailors that had protected him with a wide, boastful smile. "Go and tell the crew that we have bested the Living Reef. Tell them that we sail with warriors!"

~ ~ ~

The Beauty of the Sea

The rest of that first day, the crew rejoiced. Though there was still work to be had, the faces that had been timid were hard set now. The three heroes and Besting's two brave fighters had given the crew hope that they would survive out in the perilous waters.

Shawn took to the celebrations with expected mirth, and even Taunauk cracked a smile throughout the day. Helesys… Helesys tried to relish the lighthearted air.

But her eyes rarely left the sea. Even had she and Taunauk been alone on the ship, her gaze would've been the same. The difference now was the others looked to her, others that were not her companions, others that could not save themselves from danger. Others that relied on her.

In those moments that her eyes drifted back to the ship and the crew, she noticed that Taunauk and Shawn were also scouring the waves. They understood the newfound burden—if no one else did.

The other two fighters were Ricar and Elaine, both humans. Ricar was young and squat, with thin facial hair that made him look younger rather than older. He made a point of trying to talk to Taunauk, though Helesys did not overhear about what, exactly. From a distance, Ricar looked as if he might've been Taunauk's son. Elaine was the captain's second, even though she looked like she could be his senior. She was lithe; her face with thin wrinkles, and her steps were cunning—as if she had lived her whole life on the sea.

Helesys found herself looking at them in idle moments, searching the two sailor's faces. Wondering if they were equals to be looked to in dire events, or more that would need shielding. It was a fool's idea to measure the caliber of a warrior from afar, but a curiosity she could not slake.

~

The blaring heat of the day passed and their self-imposed watch burned long into the evening. It wasn't until the moon was high above them that Helesys contemplated sleep. By then, lanterns were lit: One at the helm and one to either side of the ship. Elaine took the helm and kept the ship steady with a small compass. Captain Besting insisted that the small night watch would be enough until morning.

Still, Helesys's eyes drifted across the dark waves, moonlight glinting off their curves. It wasn't until Taunauk laid a hand on her weary shoulder that she snapped out of it.

"Come," he said. "The ship and the sea will still be there in the morning. Or they will not, and we shall be elsewhere."

Reluctantly, she followed the outlander.

Across the deck, Shawn was staring up at the moon with wide-eyed wonder, like he'd never seen such a thing before.

Moonlight played off the rogue's face as if he were as amorphous and changing at the ocean waves.

"Is there something up there?" Helesys asked as they paused beside Shawn.

"It is nothing," he said quietly, still gazing upward. "*We are but dreams, born across the rolling sea. Slick as moonlight, pale as cream. No more than chance or mortal lapse—worldly inconsistencies.*"

Taunauk glanced upward at the moon, following Shawn's gaze, but Helesys stared at the rogue and searched his meaning. It sounded like poetry.

"I didn't take you for the poetic type," Helesys said playfully.

Shawn half-smiled, his entrancement faltering for only a moment. "Neither did I, but then we all have our moments. Don't we?"

"I suppose so," she replied. "Do you remember where the lines are from?"

The rogue shook his head, then turned from the moon to her. "I think it's about dreams, but I don't have any idea where it's from. Poetry from a half-remembered life. Funny, the things we remember."

"Come," Taunauk said. He waved and walked away. "We need rest. There will be many more nights to stare as the moon grows full. More time to wax poetical."

Shawn turned in surprise. "Did you just—"

But Taunauk was already at the stairs. He shrugged his massive shoulders and disappeared below deck.

Helesys chuckled and continued, "Make a moon joke? I think he did."

Shawn shook his head in disbelief. "He's full of surprises."

Then the two followed their comrade down below decks to the hammocks, softly lit by three half-hooded lanterns.

Helesys wrapped herself in her cloak, laid in her hammock, and listened to the soft churn of waves and faint snoring. It was only then, as she was drifting off to sleep, arms folded across her stomach, that she felt the faintest hum from her wand-arm.

It wasn't a warning. It was merely recognition that there was some magic afoot here—perhaps there had been ever since she'd stepped foot on the ship.

The weaver resolved to dwell on it tomorrow. After all, they and the ship would still be there. Or they wouldn't.

~

The next morning, the three awoke with the crew, went above deck and found the sky already blue. On the horizon, cliffs loomed. Their pale faces slicing the world in half, dividing the cloudy sky and the rolling blue of the sea. Though some of the crew were climbing the rigging and adjusting the sails, most were entranced by the sight of the cliffs and gathered at the bow to look upon them.

"We sail toward the cliffs!" Captain Besting called over the deck. "We will search for a way through the Ring of the World."

Few of the crew shared his spirits. Most were solemn. *How impossible it must feel to them*, Helesys thought, *those that didn't have the gifts of the warrior or the mage, to be trapped in a place like this.*

Helesys and Taunauk spent much of the day on watch, while Shawn worked the sails. And when the sky was blue and bright, and the cliffs had grown large in the distance, they came upon a small archipelago. Three islands, each ringed with sandy beaches and dotted with fern trees and lush grasses.

Crew were filing out from below decks to look and before long the deck was covered with all the passengers of the *Malorienta*. Helesys and Taunauk stood at the edge of the railing, while Shawn and the riggers looked on from their vantage point above.

The stout warrior Ricar called to Captain Besting, "Seems like a fine place to anchor, sir! How about that? They might have some game on the islands."

All eyes were on the islands. Ricar might've been right. The islands were smaller than Helesys thought was possible—as the limits of the sandy shores were visible from afar—yet there was much that seemed hidden by foliage. They might have hidden something better than that grass soup to eat.

But Besting did not approach the islands directly. He rounded the shore of the first. And as the crew grew quiet, even the wind and the waves seemed to die.

"Look," Taunauk whispered. Movement in the foliage.

A group of Terrans walked out from the ferns and onto the beach. They stared back at the ship and the crew. They wore simple furs, no more than drapery, and so half of their bodies were uncovered. Their hair in braids. Even from afar, Helesys could see the supple curves of the women and the men, each strong, youthful—beautiful. This was a strange thought to Helesys, since attraction had so fleetingly entered her mind since she'd been reborn in the dungeon.

Murmurs and gasps swept over the crew, and those who did not mutter in awe looked on with open mouths.

More groups began to gather on the beach. The number of the natives steadily rising to the dozens. They all stood motionless, looking back with blank stares.

Helesys's gauntlet churned with warning, snapping her from the trance. There was something too charming, too spellbinding, in the natives. Something magical and nefarious.

"They're dangerous," Helesys said. When no one moved around her, Helesys turned and said, "They are dangerous—"

Taunauk was beside her still, but his mouth was hanging open and eyes wide. Many of the men and women—nearly all—had the same entranced expression. The few children onboard tugged at their parents' sleeves and shouted for their attention—their intuition telling them the same. Only two other adults on the deck, an older man and a young woman, were moving at all, and their concern rose to shouts.

Then the ship's nose began to turn toward the island. Helesys spun and looked back toward Captain Besting at the helm with the same charmed look.

"Nope, nope, nope. Helesys! I've seen enough pretty monsters and spirits to know where this is going."'" Shawn shouted from above. The rogue somersaulted to the deck, landing with a roll. He extended a hand to her, reaching through the crowd. She took his hand and slipped through the jumbled mass. "That bloody Besting is going to run us aground."

Helesys pointed toward the captain. "Go for the helm. Steer us away from here. I'll try to erase their hold on the crew."

Shawn took off toward the back of the ship, pushing past and knocking over stunned crew—most of whom stood and went back to their mindless staring.

The weaver looked past the crew to the people—the creatures—on the shore. She churned power, meaning to counter their spell, but never had she negated so many spells nor on so many targets at once. She compounded the arcane power in her gauntlet from hum to whine to rattle, and the ancient words came to her.

"Oculis clausa et frigida corda!"

The power escaped her gauntlet and washed over the deck in an invisible wave. She had hoped to free some of the crew from the creatures' magic—any at all—but the crew stood, unmoved, like defiant trees in a storm surge.

"Stercus," she cursed, and churned power again.

The deck shuddered beneath her feet. The *Malorienta* lurched to the right, away from the island. Shawn was at the helm, and Besting had been knocked across the deck. If the crew could not be freed, they would sail away from the island, for the hold of magic had limits.

The briefest thought of the Wolf-King crossed her mind: That he had taken control of the wizard, Amadeus, from across the realms and inside the wizard's own warded sanctum. But these creatures were not the Wolf-King; they were not God here.

But before Helesys could breathe in relief of escape, a terrible sound rose up from the shore. Overlapping otherworldly voices, somewhere between rattling chains and whining glass. It was the music of the lost and the damned, that speaks to even those who do not have ears to hear it. And in her head Helesys heard the echoing of voices translated, spilling over one another like discordant waves.

"Jump overboard and be with us."

Helesys's eyes were wide with the dreadful words. The first line of men went overboard before Helesys could say the words, *"Restu sonmuvo, kompatindaj maristoj."*

Against greater foes, the holding spell resulted in a psychic battle of wills, but on the deck of the *Malorienta*, Helesys was the greater. She felt the entranced minds of the crew, cowering between the magic of the creatures and the magic of the weaver—their fear was potent and primal, and Helesys felt shame that there was no other way to save them.

She felt the cold of the sea, tasted salt and the terror of the men overboard, sinking beneath the waves. She felt them touch the sandy bottom and stare up at the flickering sky. Felt the burning in their lungs that spread to their muscles. Saw the blurry shadow of the ship's silhouette sailing away. And they could not even scream—Helesys held them so tightly, afraid to let go of one, lest her hold slip and more crew jump overboard.

And she felt one man pushing against her, one man walking to the edge of the deck. The only one that was strong enough to fight her hold when her power was divided among so many. Taunauk pushed past the frozen onlookers until he was nearly at the railing.

In the shared mindscape of the holding spell, Helesys could feel the eyes of the creatures on the shore. Hungry and thirsting for mortals—and the completeness of their desperation caused Helesys to shudder. Never before had she felt such desperation and utter lack. It wasn't merely a parched throat, rumbling stomach, or forgotten loins. It was all of those things, and feeling as if there were half of a whole. As if the creature's heart beat in another's chest and they were desperate to find who it was.

The creatures were all staring at Helesys; their desperation turned to anger and their blank faces twisted into sneers. Even though the *Malorienta* was turned and sailing directly away, Helesys could still see them staring.

She felt Taunauk step onto the railing, but in her shock, she could not utter the words. She could not trade so many lives for one, could she? Helesys did not even have the chance to breathe before her friend jumped overboard. Taunauk fell into the waves.

She ran toward the captain's deck in a mad dash, stooping to grab one of the spare lengths of rope that lay on the planks and nearly tumbling over in the process. She sprinted up the stairs, past Shawn and frozen Captain Besting, mouth hanging open as they sailed away from the beautiful monsters on the shore. Helesys looped one end of the rope around the corner post and made a slipknot, all the while keeping her eyes on the small, fading froth that marked Taunauk's descent beneath the waves.

"What are you doing?" Shawn called from the helm.

Helesys lashed the other end to her waist. Some three dozen feet separated the two ends, and the *Malorienta* was picking up speed.

She said, "Be ready in case the spell drops."

"What are you talking about?" He asked, but Helesys didn't have the time to explain. In those scant moments, she had already lost grip on the first men who went overboard. They were gone, lost to the waves.

Then Helesys plunged into the water.

Blessedly, the water was clear enough to see Taunauk's motionless body, arms wide and sinking toward the blackness. She felt her control on the sailors loosen like she were holding onto a slick ledge. Still, she dove down, swimming with desperate pulls.

Helesys grasped a handful of his cloak first. Unhooked the clasp around his neck. Then grasped the stilled barbarian from behind, her mundane arm under his arm and around his chest to grasp the neck of his chainmail vest. And as she felt the surface fade—with it, her grasp of the other sailors; she bolstered her strength and pulled with her gauntlet.

Close to Taunauk and using the holding spell, she felt his turmoil: Not bottled rage, but a quiet, terrible fear of drowning. It was powerlessness unlike anything the barbarian had ever felt. Something that even his practice of bottling emotions could not silence. Compared to the fear he expressed at the holding spell, both from Matron Mildé and now Helesys, the fear of drowning blotted it out like the sun overpowering a candle. So Helesys kept her magic divided between keeping her hold on Taunauk so that he would not struggle and bolstering her strength to haul him to the surface.

By the time they crested the surface, her muscles and lungs burned, and she gulped desperately for air. Her eyes were blurry with salt water. Shouts echoed from above, and for a moment, visions crossed her mind of men leaping off the back of the ship.

"Hold on!" Shawn shouted over the fray.

The rope rose, Helesys and Taunauk with it, pulling them out of the water and up to the captain's deck. The crew grabbed both of them and pulled them over the railing. Helesys felt the struggle fade from Taunauk, and she relinquished the magical hold. The barbarian rolled to his hands and knees and heaved salt water and bile on the deck.

They rose to shaking feet some moments later and saw the eyes of the crew upon them, a mix of fear and uncertainty. Captain Besting and Shawn stood beside them with solemn looks on their faces. Elaine was at the helm, back to them, and head bowed as she kept the ship steady. Ricar was not among the faces.

So many eyes, Helesys thought, *yet fewer than before.*

"Go on," Captain Besting called over the crew. "Get back to your stations. We'll say prayers and blessings at nightfall."

~ ~ ~

The Ring of the World

Nightfall came swiftly as the *Malorienta* approached the cliffs. The pale face of rock rose up and up, to treacherous, impossible heights—reminding Helesys of the awe she felt at the Infinite Wall. She felt like her eyes had to stretch to even take in the sight of it, that even contemplating it was a staggering act.

The crew was paralyzed much the same by the majesty. It was a small blessing, for it occupied their minds in the quiet moment when the wind was constant and the waves were small. It kept them from thinking too much of those unfortunate souls who leapt from the deck.

At least until nightfall.

In spite of the infinite dimensions of the cliffs—Captain Besting steered them toward the solitary passage through. It seemed a trick of the eyes at first, but the passage—only twice the width of the *Malorienta*—cut through to orange sunset on the other side. Whether by feat or stroke of luck, few of the crew questioned it.

Captain Besting anchored the ship two hundred feet from the cliffside. As the sun set, the imposing cliffs around them turned from white to gray and nearly to black. Once night was completely upon them, the cliffs were marked only by the absence of stars.

That was when the sobs started. They spread quietly through the ship like a plague or like a leak springing somewhere deep in the ship. Twice, curses were muttered as Helesys passed; these she pretended not to hear. It was a mark of the living to mourn, whether it looked like grief or anger. But one… one passing remark by Elaine had hurt more than all the rest.

Helesys, Taunauk, and Shawn took their meal at the bow of the ship. Alone and in silence for a time.

Shawn broke it, as was becoming of him. "You did good back there," he said with a subtle glance to Helesys.

The weaver scoffed. "It was an act of desperation. I fear it has turned the crew against me."

"Sometimes the needs of the many outweigh the needs of the few." Shawn said the words half-heartedly, without the conviction the statement required. The rogue would not even meet her eyes as he said them.

Helesys recalled the few words uttered by Elaine—the remark said plainly, yet that cut more deeply than any other words could have:

"*Ricar could swim*," Helesys repeated. "I do not know about the others, but Ricar could swim."

Helesys felt like she was holding the men again with magic, feeling their despair as they slipped beneath the waves. But in the turmoil of those moments, she had not felt the quiet confusion of Ricar—

"Do not trouble yourself," Taunauk said quietly. "You did what you must and the decision has passed. No amount of emotion or magic will change what has happened."

Helesys heard the words, but she was staring off across the sea.

Shawn asked, "Is that a barbarian—um, outlander—sentiment?"

Taunauk nodded and set aside his empty bowl. "The Endroggen think as much. Anger, sorrow, happiness… Use them to carry you forward, rather than to hold you back." Taunauk met Shawn's wide eyes, and added, "Use them as wind for your sails, not an anchor."

The rogue smiled and waved a hand. "I understood the first explanation."

"Oh."

Taunauk turned to Helesys, and she met his eyes, ready for whatever wisdom he had for her—as if he had already not said enough. "Thank you," was all Taunauk said.

Helesys smiled wearily, earnestly, and felt the sinking feeling of her actions pass. They became a shadow, rather than a weight, and in the cool night air she was glad to be sitting with her comrades. No matter how far the ship sailed, their camaraderie would take them farther.

"It's never easy," Shawn mused idly. "It couldn't be a pleasure cruise."

Footsteps behind them. "It very nearly was," said Captain Besting. He sat across from them, and Helesys had to turn to see him.

It was not lost on her that the captain never sat or stood too close to the railings

The rogue asked, "What do you mean, it nearly was?"

"Dark pleasures lined the shore back there, boy. Those were pleasure demons. Gods, I knew, and I still couldn't bring myself to steer away fast enough."

Taunauk asked, "Are they a *lingering* death? One that traps a Terran's soul?"

Besting shook his head. "No."

"Perhaps you should've let me go," Taunauk said cheekily.

"They're also cannibals," Besting added. "First, they lure Terrans in with temptations of the flesh, then they feed on your emotions. Meat is last, when you're too tired and brain-dead to fight back."

Taunauk shrugged. "There are worse ways to go."

Shawn said with a longing look. "You had me in the first half. You really did."

Helesys chuckled and waved her elven hand. "You men are pigs. The whole lot of you."

Laughter caught them like a sudden flame, one barely contained and stifled quickly so it did not get out of hand.

When the moment passed and began to smolder, Besting said, "There is something I need to tell you. Air that needs clearing. This is not my first voyage. I've sailed many times in my life before, and I've sailed many times in this life."

Helesys, Taunauk, and Shawn exchanged distraught glances. Taunauk replied, "Speak plainly."

Besting held up a hand to stay them. "Just as you are trapped in this prison, my men and I are trapped on this ship. We were bound to the *Malorienta* long before we were swallowed up and landed on these shores. We have never made it to the ends, never to freedom. Each time we sink we wind up back on these shores with the *Malorienta*. Do not worry, you are not bound to the ship in life nor in death. Nor are any new crew that sail with us. Nor do my crew wake up in any other worlds. It's as if neither the cursed ship nor the cursed place are willing to part with the souls they have claimed."

Helesys was taken aback by this realization, as were Taunauk and Shawn. She said, "It makes sense now how you found so much wood for repairs when trees were scarce upon the beach. And how you seemed to know of the Living Reef and how you found this cut through the cliffs. You've been here before, haven't you?" Besting nodded in confirmation.

She was suddenly aware of the quiet humming in her gauntlet. Had she mistaken it for nearby danger all this time when the wand had been trying to tell her of the ship itself?

Shawn asked, "So, why didn't you avoid the siren shore?"

Besting shrugged. "Their spell is powerful, even without singing. Dark pleasures and all that."

"Aye," Shawn replied, as if hypnotized by the siren's call, then quickly turned to Helesys. "So… Why were you and I immune to it?"

Taunauk grunted. "A good question."

Besting said, "A handful of souls are immune to the siren's call, but they are no help. They don't know why or don't remember, or they will not speak of those things."

Helesys shrugged. "I'm sorry, but I do not have an answer. I do not remember much. I am elven and of noble birth, but the rest is forgotten. Besting, I hesitate to ask but… What dangers wait for us here?"

The captain looked to the starless black sky—the hole in the night where the cliffs blotted out the heavens. "It always ends here. We've never made it past the cliffs."

"What dangers?" Taunauk repeated.

The captain sighed. "There are rocks below the water—I can steer us through, but there are rocks that fall from above. The very world quakes to stop us."

Helesys nodded. "I will take care of the falling rocks."

But Besting's eyes had fallen from the cliff to the sea, as if something were dragging his gaze overboard and into the pitch black. Everyone noticed.

Shawn simply said, "Tell us what else is out there."

"I hoped we'd sail through before sunset, but I need good light to see. That is why we stopped. We will all spend the night below decks. Barricade the stairs and hide in the hold. They will come from the depths and overrun the ship." Besting's voice had dropped to a whisper as he spoke, as if merely talking about the creatures would draw their attention to the ship. "The *eels* will come tonight." Besting stood quickly and shivered in the night air.

Helesys asked, "What would you have us do?"

"Pray to whatever gods you believe in that they don't make it through the barricades."

~

Captain Besting called for all crew to follow him below deck, even the nightwatch. Helesys, Taunauk, and Shawn followed the procession of confused sailors. Crew below deck were already lugging heavy crates and barrels up the stairs, piling them at base of both sets of stairs—the initial set that led to the crew's quarters and the second that led to the hold.

Once everyone was below deck, the crew stacked the barricades so that the mass of objects was tightly packed, covered the last three stairs, and spilled out onto the floor. They were impressive barricades, but did not assuage the growing pit in Helesys's stomach. If anything, they added to it, calling into question what kind of terrible creatures the thorough measures were keeping out, and just how numerous they would be if Besting was leaving no souls above deck.

Several of the nightwatch voiced concern at being below decks, but the captain merely said that deep waters were dangerous and that they were better below decks. This was not enough to quench the whispers that crew like a fire across the ship. Soon murmurs about the eels reached Helesys and the others.

By the time the second barricade was finished and all the crew was stowed in the hold, that final compartment of the ship had a large opening, bare of crates. Most of the crew mulled in this opening, slumped against each other or against the remaining stores. Others had strewn blankets across the rest of the cargo.

Down here, the embers of concern threatened to catch into hysteria. Some of the crew were sobbing. Mothers held and quieted children while they themselves had blank stares. Two little girls hid in the shelves, silently.

As the final barrels were moved into place, Helesys wondered how many of them had lived through this particular horror and which were at the mercy of the rumors and their own imaginations.

Captain Besting stepped in front of the crowd and rubbed his hands together in slow, nervous swirls. "Some of you are wondering why we're down here. Some of you already know. Tonight, the hold is the safest place in the ship. The walls are thick and we've packed the stairs tight so nothing can get down here.

"The eels come up from the depths with the rising moon. You'll hear them scratching at the hull as they climb. They will be looking for us, but they won't find us. Not down here. We'll stay nice and quiet, and in a few hours the eels will go back down into the depths. We will stay here until morning."

For those moments and a little while after, it seemed as if Besting had quenched their worries. Elaine and some of the other sailors handed blankets to the children and told them to cover their ears.

Then one of the children hiding on the shelves screamed, eyes wide and looking across the hold—past the crates and to the last corners of barrels and boxes.

Helesys churned power while her comrades drew blades. They were around the corner before the end of the child's breath, weapons leveled.

In the shadows of the farthest corner of the hold, where the bow of the boat began to curve upward, they saw a single, massive yellow eye. The dark, vertical pupil fixated on the heroes and it squinted at the sight of them. The reptilian face smiled to reveal dozens of pin-shaped teeth—smiled in recognition.

"Hello again," Pitiful Lull said in a raspy voice, careful to keep itself half-hidden behind the crates. It rapped grotesquely long fingers on a barrel—one several feet away. Helesys pictured its abnormally long, spiny limbs folded like bat wings to fit inside such a space.

"You," Taunauk and Shawn whispered in surprise.

"I assure you, he is harmless," Captain Besting said from beside them. He repeated this again to the huddle crew, but quiet gasps continued despite it. Then to the heroes he said, "Lull's been here as long as we have. Ever since we first woke up on this shore."

"How is that possible?" Helesys asked. "We saw him in the rusted prison."

"As did I," Shawn said. "Just last death, in fact. Do you remember what we talked about?"

Lull's puss-yellow eye narrowed further. "What kind of question is that? I am not that Lull."

Shawn shook his head in frustration. "You told me about the wizard, Amadeus. You were his apprentice… I think I understand your accident now. Amadeus was trying to escape. In the old man's experimentations, your soul was split and scattered across the realms. That is how Lull can be both here and in flooded caverns."

Lull nodded quickly. "The dark one speaks the truth. I am not that Lull, and he is not me. But…" The reptilian lips trailed off.

Helesys said calmly, "Tell us."

The creature stared at her now, eye wide and mesmerizing in the shadows. "I dream. I dream of what the other me's have seen. I remember meeting you two and then you," Lull said, pointing to each of them in turn. "But it is half-remembered—they are coming!" Lull ducked behind the crates.

~

Silence fell over the cargo hold as the crew waited—it seemed some were so still they were afraid to breathe. Only an occasional shiver or moan of despair lingered.

Helesys, Taunauk, and Shawn stalked back over to the foot of the stairs, to the barricade.

Somewhere in the black of night and freezing water, soft churns and swishes sounded. They came by the dozens, the sounds as soft as a breeze. Then came scraping sounds that Besting had foretold of—each was a soft thump, followed by long draws of nails or teeth upon the wooden hull. These came from higher up, near the waterline, and Helesys imagined the eels swimming to the surface and then climbing the planks.

The scraping grew and grew, until the sounds wrapped around the deck—surrounding them, echoing through the planks of the *Malorienta*, louder, like some ghastly chorus rising to a crescendo as more of the creatures came for them. Soft thumps of flesh sounded above them like drum beats—as the creatures spilled over onto the main deck.

Scraping sounds grew again, this time echoing down the hall. The sound of nails on wood and also wood on wood— the creatures beat against the first barricade. Crates and barrels thumped against the floor as they pushed past the barricade. Followed by wet thumps again as the creatures spilled onto the crew deck—just above them.

Shawn pointed to the floor of the cargo hold. Water trickled down the stairs to the room and was pooling at their feet. Too slow to be a leak and too viscous to be *just* salt water.

Above them, the creatures hissed in short bursts like the sound of shrill steam. Tearing sounds—of rope and hammocks being ripped and eaten. Then ghastly scraping, this time in machine-quick bursts, like metal gears winding up at a terrible speed. These sounds came and went in an instant, yet each sounding sent shivers along Helesys's spine.

Helesys peered through cracks in the cargo hold barricade, trying to look up the stairs to glimpse the creatures.

In the gloom, a snake-like head slithered into view. Its head was nearly a perfect circle, flat on the face. It had no eyes, nor nose—the only feature on the flat face were four rows of concentric teeth, and a fleshy throat in the center. The creature slithered all the way to the crest of the stairs and Helesys saw the alien body in earnest: The head tapered down to a body that was rope-thin, and the body stretched out to half-a-dozen arms—or rather, heads—each with the same circular teeth-ringed face. The heads pushed and slithered like blind serpents.

The eel slithered and plopped down the stairs, and once stopped to investigate the wall of the narrow staircase. Its mouth flexed and the teeth began to pulse back and forth. It plunged its face against the wall, and that head of the creature shook violently as its teeth ground against the wood. When the creature's grip slackened, it revealed a three-ringed gouge in the wall.

Images flashed through Helesys's mind of the creatures biting and tearing flesh off in similar cylindrical bites. Images she pushed aside with a kindling of power.

Someone—Shawn—tapped her shoulder. Rather than speak, he mouthed, "*What is it?*"

She glared and mouthed back for him to *be quiet.*

Taunauk had stowed his battleaxe and his shield on the ground beside them. He crouched and braced himself against the back of the crates. Then motioned for Shawn and Helesys to do the same. They each braced against the barricade as quietly as possible. The rest of the crew waited—some wide eyed and gripping weapons tightly, others huddled and shaking quietly behind the few crates that were left. Captain Besting and Elaine were among the brave.

The eel slithered all the way down to the barricade and bit against it, each time making some of the crew flinch.

The crates lurched and Helesys bolstered her strength. She dug her heels against the deck and strained to keep from slipping. Taunauk's muscles flexed in similar surprise—Shawn nearly fell backward. The eel pushed again, twice more, before it stopped.

Slithering above them and the gnarled head of the eel squeezed through one of the openings between the barrels and the ceiling. Whimpers echoed through the hold as the crew tried to move away from the creature. Helesys reached up with her gauntlet and grasped the neck of the beast, just behind the head. It was nearly too thick around for her to hold, but it was close enough to the mouth that it couldn't turn to bite her. The circular mouth spasmed and pulsed its teeth, dripping thick mucus onto the deck beside the mage.

At the top of the stairway, the wet gathering sounds of more eels.

"Hold it still," Taunauk said. The barbarian grabbed his axe and swung neatly at the base of the eel's neck. The tension and the fight went out of the creature almost instantly and blue blood sprayed in thick droplets on the surrounding crates. The eel slumped back onto the other side of the stairs.

The mass of eels, sensing blood, rolled down the stairs in waves. The blind creatures began devouring their injured comrade, and the horrid sounds of scraping and tearing of flesh filled the cargo hold. Helesys tossed the severed head of the creature through the hole and as far up the stairs as she could. Then she laid her gauntlet through the hole and took aim at half a dozen more creatures—careful of power and direction—and blasted up the stairs, turning them into a feast for the horde.

A deafening cacophony followed as the eels turned on their wounded brethren. Of tearing flesh and spilling blood, punctuated by the horrid machine-quick scraping of teeth on the wood—of a frenzied eel lashing out and missing a wounded brother. The smell of bile filled the ship. So thick was the violence that blue blood began spilling down the stairs, the consistency of sludge.

The crew huddled with closed ears and silent prayers. Some of the kids screamed—Helesys was sure of it—but their voices were drowned out by slaughter. Even though the carnage seemed contained to the crew deck above, Helesys, Taunauk, and Shawn held their backs to the barricade, lest the chaos spill down onto the stairs.

Minutes passed, and when the violence lulled, Helesys fired more shots up the stairs, bursting eels, and starting the cycle of viciousness anew. Anything to keep the creatures distracted.

There was no peace that night—not until the sun crested the horizon. Only then did the creatures slither back down to the depths. Splashes sounded outside as the eels hurled themselves outside, back toward the hellish depths. Only then did the crew breathe measured sighs of relief.

~

When the morning colors filtered down to the cargo hold, the crew began clearing the barricades. Then Helesys, Taunauk, and Shawn carefully climbed up the stairs to the carnage of the crew deck.

The violence had gone on so long that night, that Helesys thought herself immune to the gruesome scene and to the smell. She was wrong on both counts.

The crew deck was covered in the sludge of dead eels. The blue blood was thick with chunks of half-ground flesh and peppered with teeth—seemingly the only thing the creatures wouldn't eat of their own. Helesys kindled her wand-arm so she didn't spit up, but even with her constitution bolstered, the air felt as thick as fog and she couldn't push away the thought of it.

Beside her, Taunauk walked stoically through the gore and around the corners, axe drawn. His heavy boots squelched as he walked. As he checked for any still-living beasts.

"Movernus's bones—" Shawn muttered before gagging viciously and running up to the main deck for air.

Most of the crew had the same reaction to the scene. Children closed their eyes and were carried across it. All wanted desperately to get up to the main deck, breathe fresh air, and feel cool wind upon their faces. None but Pitiful Lull stayed below decks.

Cleaning up took the better part of the morning. Those who had the stomach for it went below and slopped gore into buckets. Those who didn't stayed above deck and tossed the buckets overboard. Only a dozen had the former duty—Helesys, Taunauk, and Elaine among them. Shawn and the extra hands above spent the rest of their time checking rigging. Twice during clean up, Helesys saw the spindly fingers of Pitiful Lull reaching up from the stairs below to grab chunks of eel, then scurry back down to the cargo hold.

At midday, they would sail through the Narrows —so perilous the passage that the *Malorienta* had never made it through.

Captain Besting took the helm and called for all able-bodied Terrans to stay on the main deck, whilst the others hid below. Elaine would take point on the bow and call out warnings to Besting about rocks beneath the surface. Shawn and the riggers would call out warnings of falling rocks. Helesys would attempt to cover the *Malorienta* from the largest falling rocks by blasting them into harmless chunks. Taunauk and the spare crew would clear the deck as fast as they could, lest the debris accumulate and sink the hull even deeper into the perilous waters.

Once Besting and Elaine had assigned everyone's duties, the captain ordered a half-sail and steered the *Malorienta* toward the Narrows. He did this somberly and without a speech to rouse the crew.

Helesys stood in the middle of the main deck. She had stowed her cloak and let the midday sun beat warmly upon her face. She breathed slowly, steadying herself. In spite of her calm appearance, she could not help but feel the captain's dread at the sight of the Narrows. The cliff faces were jagged and violent, and the water boiled between the rocks as the two sides of the massive sea were forced into the passage.

How many times could she look defiantly at death?

Once more, she thought. Always, *once more*.

Helesys kindled power and readied her gauntlet as the *Malorienta* slipped completely into the Narrows. Even from the middle of the ship, Helesys could see the occasional spire of underwater rock reaching up like a spearpoint from the churning waves. For every one that pierced the surface, half a dozen more outcroppings lay just beneath. She knew why Besting waited till the sun's pitiful crest to sail the passage—otherwise the dangers would've been completely hidden from view and the sky above them would've only allowed an hour of light to directly illuminate the water.

At the helm, Besting donned black framed goggled to better see the hidden dangers.

The crew waited, eyes darting from the water to the cliffs and back again. Helesys turned her eyes upward. The churning of the waves and rocking of the ship made the cliff sides waver in Helesys's vision and made the rough faces look alive.

The *Malorienta* was completely inside the Narrows when the cliffs began to quake. An almost imperceptible shudder built to a low groan as the cliffs shook. Rocks tumbled free from the top and from the walls, and plummeted toward them.

Helesys fired, blasting chunks of rocks as they left the walls, targeting everything larger than a Terran and showering the deck and the waves with pebbles and stone mist. Even the smaller rocks fell so far that they fell heavy against the deck. Some even splintered the boards. So when the deluge slowed, she targeted even the smaller rocks.

The crew above deck slunk from railing to post and to mast, hesitant to stay out in the open for too long. Even Taunauk, with Everfall on his back for protection, scurried across. They heaved the larger of the stones on deck and hurled them over-board. Within the first third of the passage, the deck became tumultuous as Captain Besting navigated the underwater rocks. Crew slipped and fell as the rock dust accumulated on the deck and the rocking grew more desperate. Somehow Shawn and the other riggers high above managed to keep their handholds and footing amidst the turmoil.

Helesys wand-arm grew hot with effort and constant hum of power. The weaver spun and stepped light across the deck in an untimed waltz as she turned from cliff face to cliff face, letting arcane blasts fly. In the cloudy chaos, she fell into a trance as she often did during battle. When her mind was set to task and nothing else, and all the world fell away. She trusted the memory of muscle and sinew and the mithril bindings of her wand. The arcane blasts struck true on the stones and did not sail through them—lest an errant blast strike the cliffside and cause even more destruction. Though the blasts of her gauntlet were silent, their impacts with the falling stones sounded in sharp cracks and slams. The explosions of rock be-gan to fall in time with her steps, and the weaver began her dance in earnest—one of battle trance and ballet.

And a memory came back to Helesys, one of the ballrooms of the elven great halls. Ornate wood carved with thousands of years of history, the stones of the floor older than the cities of man. A hundred elves in attendance wearing the silken dresses and suits of their ancestors and dancing to steps older than spoken language.

And in the upper reaches of the room sat a mechanical player piano, the newest and still ancient addition to the room. An arcane contraption that could play one thousand songs in perfect time and recollection. One of the only arcane contraptions allowed in such a place of ceremony—only because it allowed the musicians to dance as freely as the nobles and the crafters. The machine was the great equalizer.

Short-lived tears streamed from the corner of the weaver's eyes as she spun upon the deck. With a mix of soldier's prowess and her wand's power, her dance became one of mechanical precision, of perfect step and time. Helesys became a blur, became possessed. In the maelstrom she stood alone, and the cliffs wept their own dry tears of rock and ash because so few struck the deck of the *Malorienta*.

The world grew blue as they passed the halfway point of the chasm, and the quaking of the cliffs grew thunderous. Sharp cracks and tears echoed so loud they shook the sea, the ship, and even Helesys's chest. Whole sides of the cliff tore free—both sides taller even than masts of the *Malorienta*. So tight was the passage, there would be no way to slip past them both.

The weaver turned her gauntlet toward the right of the ship, the closest rock face, churned power deeply and let a barrage fly. Purple energy screamed at the falling rock and a dozen blasts struck true. But even pulverized, tons of rock crashed into the water and made the ship lurch in the waves. Besting and the crew were shouting—or perhaps had been the entire time—but Helesys couldn't hear them over the chaos. The scurrying crew now abandoned the deck completely, less they be battered or crushed.

Helesys whirled around, the metal of her wand-arm steaming, to the falling cliff on the left and let fly as much arcane destruction as she could. The second falling cliff splintered and finally shattered—but Helesys could not stop them all.

Two chunks from the last cliff fell hard on the left side of the ship—one shattering the railing, the other punching through the main deck and landing on the crew deck below. Even as the remaining smaller rocks pelted the deck, Taunauk ran through the hail, Everfall on his back, and down the stairs. Presumably to check for any injured.

More of the cliffs fell behind them, but it was too late—the *Malorienta* slipped through the chasm and out into the open air. The thunder of rock sounded behind the ship like applause as the crew gazed upon a horizon of blue sky and churning gray.

Helesys stood defiantly on deck. Her chest heaved for air, and her steaming gauntlet burned the mundane skin of her shoulder. She basked in the exhaustion. It would've been an easy thing to push the sensations away—to kindle power and numb the burn of her lungs and skin. But then would she feel so alive in this place of endless death?

Helesys glanced upward and saw Shawn on the topmost mast, basking in the open air.

And as the moment dawned on the rest of the crew, cheers rose and drowned out everything else.

~ ~ ~

The Living Tempest

The *Malorienta* and her crew had made it through the narrows with superficial injuries. Only some cuts and bruises, a broken railing and punctured main deck.

That night, the crew celebrated. There were only two bottles of liquor on the ship—aged brandy from Captain Besting's personal stash. Enough for each soul to have a toast. They gathered on the main deck and Besting toasted to Helesys, Taunauk, and Shawn, for getting them through the Narrows when all other times they had met a rocky doom.

For the first time, Helesys saw the quiet resignation of the crew lift. Children ran and played above deck for the first time, mindful of the damaged parts of the hull. The less able of the crew also spent the evening on deck. There was an air of freedom that had been sorely missing. The crew had spent so long in the wake of certain death that the mirth in the air was palpable.

Helesys and Taunauk sat to the bow of the ship, cross-legged on the planks. Shawn laid on his side, head propped up on his hand. Their cloaks were left below—a gesture the weaver mused on: To relax and enjoy themselves after a hard won strife. They spent a long stretch of the evening merely enjoying the setting sun, which stretched out across the water, the tiny orange circle rippling across the waves and becoming infinite. And enjoying the newfound joy onboard.

It wasn't until the sun was nearly gone and the stars appeared, that Shawn lit a lantern and broke the silence.

"They'll dream tonight," the rogue said. "They'll dream for the first time in months."

Helesys replied, "You mean that they'll remember their dreams? I thought the mind always dreamed."

Shawn shook his head and his eyes softened. "In the depths of despair, at those lowest points, the mind ceases to dream. To see them today… Those were the smiles of a people who have remembered how to dream."

Taunauk said, "You speak like a man who has been there." Of the three of them, the outlander still sat straight up, as he always did.

Shawn nodded thoughtfully. "Perhaps I have." The rogue rolled over and regarded the star-filled sky. He pointed to the half-risen moon, full and bright in the sky. "I thought about her last night. I've seen a moon in other realms, but it's not our moon—it can't be, right? There couldn't be more than one moon… How could it capture a moon?"

"It might be an illusion," Helesys added.

"Aye," Shawn said. "That is what I think, but then the sun is a lie, too. And are all the lights above false stars, then?"

Helesys leaned back against the railing and looked upon the sky anew. "Until a few moments ago, seeing the stars always filled me with hope."

"Sorry."

"Don't be," Helesys replied plainly. "I would rather know the truth, then to believe falsely." Then she told them of her memory in the Narrows—of dancing in the elven ballroom with a hundred other nobles, while a machine kept time.

When she was finished, Shawn added playfully, "There's irony there, that a machine played the music you remember so well."

She shrugged. "Truth, in a sense."

Taunauk said quietly, "Truth need not be sobering. It does not change our current path.

Footsteps approached. Captain Besting said, "Truth will only carry you so far. You will need faith and blind stubbornness for the rest." Besting groaned as he sat down across from them. His shirt was half open, revealing a bony chest. He cradled a cup two fingers full of brandy.

He continued, "I wanted to thank you personally. We wouldn't have made it through without you."

Shawn pointed to Helesys without looking at her. "Especially you. You're quite the weapon."

Helesys squinted her eyes at him, unsure of how to take his comment.

Besting nodded thoughtfully. "We've never made it through the narrows—never even come close. Quite the feat." He trailed off, leaving much unspoken. In its place, he merely looked to Helesys and said, "Thank you."

But Helesys knew. She could see the weariness in him that she had seen in so many others across the realms. Besting implied that if they perished this time, they would wake up without her. And, in all likelihood, never make it through the narrows again.

The captain sipped his brandy and sighed.

And Helesys could no longer stand the silence. "How long was it before your memories returned?"

After thinking a moment, Besting said, "A dozen deaths, I suppose, though no one remembers just how we got here. Not even the foggiest idea… Perhaps, it is a blessing that you don't remember." It was a sudden, abashed statement, and the captain hung his head.

The three heroes all turned their attention to the captain.

"I can't stand it," Helesys said quietly. "I can't stand *not knowing* the truth."

Besting turned to Helesys as he spoke. "Consider this… One of my men, Swithin Bradley, not a pinnacle or paragon of virtue, in this life or the last. In the previous life, he was angry—so angry with the world. He took it out on himself and his young boy, Flinton. Beat and berated the lad until he stowed away on a ship. On one of his more sober days, Swithin sought out a ship—my ship. He wanted desperately to make amends to his boy, but Swithin couldn't find him. Some think that Flinton went overboard or that he changed his name, that he doesn't want to see his old man.

"Then the *Malorienta* got stuck here on this cursed beach. Stubbornness and desperation are all that's all that's keeping Swithin going. Man wakes up after every death craving the drink, shaking and cursing it, and—up until tonight—thought there wasn't a drop in this world." Besting chuckled and took a drink of brandy. "These bottles, like everything else, come back every time. I'm going to have to hide the brandy now that he knows about it…

"Truth is, Swithin ain't never going to see his boy again. Stubbornness is all Swithin's got. It's probably for the best, anyhow. He'd just find a way to muck it up."

Shawn sat up, shocked, and asked, "You don't think the man's changed. Gods, how could he not?"

The captain paused, cup half raised. "Maybe he's changed—*maybe*. The wind changes, most men don't. Flinton changed because his dad beat it out of him. I've sailed with the old man for Gods know how long, and I'm telling you that even after living in this infernal place... I can't say that he's changed." Besting gestured with his glass. "I wager it can be done, but you'd have to change *now*, before your memories come back. Before the shackles and the walls of the past come back... Sometimes I fear the sea is all I will ever know again."

Besting stood in frustration and threw the cup overboard. Brandy splattered on the deck and wafted through the air, past Helesys, and was forgotten in the breeze. The captain turned to walk away, leaving Shawn confused at the outburst.

Before he was half a dozen steps away, Helesys asked, "What about you, captain? Did you change when you had the chance?"

Besting paused and turned back to them, fists clenched to steady his shaking voice. "No happy men sail on these planks. Not on the *Malorienta*. Not *here*."

Helesys watched him go. Watched him walk across the deck, past the merriment that smoldered like a dying fire, then disappear below deck, leaving them to contemplate all that they did not know. In the impossible realms, secrets weighed heavier than forgotten memories.

~

In the morning they woke to a sea no one had set eyes upon before, and the sky had grown to an ominous mix of green and gray that swirled as viciously as the sea.

Most of the crew gathered in the relative peace of the morning to bear witness. Captain Besting stood at the helm and called out over the crew and the sea. "We have lit the lamp of hope and it has burned so very bright. Gods willing, we shall cut a path through the storm and make it through to the other side. And if they do not will it this time, we shall try again and again!"

He sent the crew to shelter below deck, keeping only the necessary souls above. The sails were trimmed to their smallest margin before the riggers came down. Besting tied ropes to anchors on the decking and then lashed the other end around his waist. Helesys, Taunauk and Shawn tied a dozen other ropes around the deck for handholds, should they need to leave the captain's side.

The wind grew from a whisper to a bellow, and the waves turned to white caps. Thunder cracked the horizon as if the world was splitting at the seams.

Helesys and Shawn were to Besting's right, and Shawn called to her over the wind. "I thought a lot about the truth of it all last night. It's not the lie of it all that concerns me, it's seeing the edges of the prison. I look at the false stars and all I see are a million lights of places we will never go to."

It was a strange sentiment, and Helesys smiled at it. "A little arrogant, don't you think? That you would visit the stars."

"I had a dream last night that I visited the stars." The rogue smiled back, shrugged, and added, "I don't know what it means." Then the storm was upon them.

The wind grew to a roar and the white caps rose higher and higher. The waves were cresting above the deck, causing the

Malorienta to rise and fall twenty feet at a time. The nose of the ship pitched toward the sky and then toward the depths. Icy salt water washed across the deck at the trough of their descent, and as they crested each wave the water blasted them. Helesys kindled strength, and still her muscles burned from exertion. Her legs from balancing, her arms from holding on. Within minutes of the maelstrom, they were all soaked. Captain Besting screamed defiantly as they sailed over the first two waves, but then he fell silent as the turmoil grew. Helesys's eyes burned from the salt, and she ducked her head to breathe lest she breathe only water.

Rain pelted them from above, and each wave grew higher and each more vicious. They ducked into the trough of the wave and the next crest rose up higher than the mainmast. As the *Malorienta* climbed, the nose pitched nearly straight up, and twice Helesys's feet slipped out from under her. Water exploded over the bow and Helesys went blind as the *Malorienta* pitched downward.

The main mast snapped and then groaned. Helesys squinted through the haze and saw the top of the mast growing large. She siphoned the wand's remaining power and blasted the mast thrice, splitting it and scattering it into the waves.

Helesys wiped her eyes, and opened them to find the sky and the storm gone, and a wall of water in its place—as high as the Infinite Wall. The *Malorienta* pitched up, defiantly trying to climb it, but the crest of the wave was already curling over— falling toward them.

The *Malorienta* pitched up and up and then over backwards. The world itself seemed to flip. Helesys closed her eyes. Even with all her power bolstering her, she lost track of everything.

She was underwater, fumbling for the rope, for the ship, for her comrades, and found nothing. Helesys tumbled over and over, not knowing which way was up. The sky was gone. Air was gone. Her wand-arm burned hot to keep her conscious. Her lungs burned, distant, dull and creeping.

She thought desperately of the seams she opened in the Apothecary's realm, that she might tear one open and escape drowning. But as Helesys felt blindly for the magic that binded the realm, she grasped nothing.

Instead, Helesys found flashes of memories: Of serpents lining the stonework of Great House Byyra. Of her mother and her sister, Wynbella and Aradi. Helesys took shears and cut her own long hair in front of them. It was an act of defiance—she felt this, knew this. She pledged to join the legion—the elven military.

Helesys stomach wrenched as she lost herself in the memory. Her mother's face was warm in spite of her daughter's rebellion—of joining the legion against her wishes. Aradi, her sister, was smiling—one of playful encouragement and yet... it belied something else: The quietest flicker of sinister notion.

In the cold, swirling ocean, the candle went out from inside her.

~ ~ ~

Meridian

Helesys opened her eyes and realized she was face down in the sand.

She rose and saw dunes stretching out to every horizon but one. Behind her, the smallest sliver of ocean could be seen. The sky was colored white by a haze of clouds, so thick that there was only the faintest hint of blue. The wind blew softly, fluttering her cloak.

The weaver looked at the shoulders of her cloak, then down at her dry and mended clothes. Had her fumbling for the seams of the realm worked? Or had she been reborn here instead of in the hallway?

Helesys *appeared* to be alone on the dunes, yet she felt the presence of something. And when it spoke, she felt the voice come from all around, from all directions, from below her in the sand, from above in the sky, and even from within her.

"*Weaver, wanderer, prisoner… I have brought you here to the world between. Helesys Byyra, I need your help.*"

Helesys listened carefully, but couldn't discern more from the voice—not even whether it was male or female, or even

Terran. The voice seemed to waiver between high and low pitched, and even to mechanical and musical notes.

And so Helesys asked the obvious question, "Who, or what, are you?"

"In time, all will be revealed. Only know that, for now, our goals align. You seek to escape. I seek the death of the Wolf-King. They are one in the same."

The weaver listened with half-closed eyes. She focused on her wand, hoping that it would offer some other insight that her eyes and ears could not, but the wand was silent. There was no hum of magic nor of warning.

"You ask the impossible of us. I've seen what he can do and our power is no match… Not yet. Can you help us?"

"I already aid you. It is by my will and with my gift that you bring back relics across death. But I shall offer you another… You are right that the Wolf-King is above your power and that you will need more relics. Seek all that you can find, and then seek one more. For the most powerful relic lies at the bottom of the endless sea, miles beneath the surface. The Machine of Antrikaumora"

Helesys listened, but her mind reeled. Was this the gate-keeper? Why did she seek the Wolf-King's death? But all that she uttered was, "You must tell me your name."

"For both our sakes, I cannot. He is listening."

Helesys shivered at the thought of the Wolf-King. "Then tell me how to reach the relic at the bottom of the sea."

"You must travel back. Seek the wizard, Zhug, and his treasure horde. Travel back by death or by seam."

Before Helesys could ask another question, she felt the sand drop from beneath her feet. Felt the sensation of falling or of flying—though neither her mind nor her gut could tell the difference.

The world was awash in color again. The sky was blue and the waters a swirling gray and white. And Helesys saw it all from above as the shoreline passed underneath her. The *Malorienta* lay on the shore, battered and yet not completely broken. The crew were already piecing her back together with her scattered timbers. Though she could not make them out from so high up, there was no doubt Captain Besting and the others were alive again.

And then the world went black.

~

The next thing Helesys knew was falling.

She crouched into a roll and then knelt on the stone. The first room of the dungeon flickered with torchlight. Taunauk landed heavy beside her and the weaver breathed a sigh of relief. She rose, took in the dusty sight of that first room, and noticed that once again, Shawn was not with them. The rogue seemed to orbit them, as if swinging next to them in one life and ebbing away from them in the next. He would come again, and at least she wasn't alone.

She met Taunauk's eyes and found them wide with concern. So Helesys asked, "Did you see something? Or speak to something?"

Taunauk nodded to both. He recounted the same experience of waking up on the dunes, on the plane between, and speaking to the disembodied voice. And as they recounted their experience, Helesys was overcome by the eeriness of the similarities—of the questions asked and answers given:

The voice who-would-not-be-named asked for their help to defeat the Wolf-King. Told them to seek Zhug's treasure for something that would deliver them to the bottom of the endless sea. That down in the depths they would find *The Machine of Antrikaumora*, the key to defeating the Wolf-King. That somehow, escaping and the death of the Wolf-King aligned. Lastly, the voice revealed to be the one aiding them—the one granting them the power to bring relics across the realms after death.

The difference was that Taunauk had thought to ask *why*. Of all the trapped beings, why had the voice chosen Helesys, Taunauk, and Shawn?

It gave the same cryptic answer: *In time, all will be revealed.*

Helesys sighed in frustration. "This place delights in suffering." She kicked at a loose stone and sent it rolling across the floor.

Taunauk shrugged. "That is likely."

The weaver's mind turned back toward the fleeting memories she glimpsed before death. To her sister Aradi's disquieting smile. Helesys pushed away the memory of her sister and reached for her long hair—metal hand retracing the memory of shearing it off. The metal phased through the length of it and caused the illusion to flicker. Her real hair was short—barely past her chin.

"I think it is a noble fashion to want to keep it long," she said.

Taunauk waited in respectful silence for her to continue.

A moment later, she shared her brief memories with him, about cutting her hair, the feelings toward her mother and sister, and their remembered names. And that she joined the elven military.

But the memories wore on her and she needed to push them away. She asked, "What of you? Do you remember anything?"

Taunauk nodded and bowed his head in thought. "I remember a feast. Then I remember leaving my clan and taking the title of Aonar. I... I don't remember why."

"It seems like an honor to send you off like that."

This time, he nodded reluctantly. "It is. But I feel it was an unwelcome one. A burden equal in weight."

"Could you have refused it?"

Taunauk smirked, and the expression was gone as quick as it appeared. "That is not our way. Endroggen do what is asked of them. We do what we must for the clan. I feel it was a necessary task. A worthy task..."

Her comrade seemed to reach his limits, his otherwise stoic demeanor cracking, and she felt the need to reassure him. "In time, you will remember. *We* will remember." She waved her mundane hand for them to begin their journey through the realm.

Taunauk nodded, then readied Everfall and axe. "To task." The barbarian led the way down the dim hallway and the weaver followed.

~ ~ ~

NEXT TIME ON
*A BATTLEAXE AND
A METAL ARM*
Book 8:

Path of the Forgotten
Available November 2021

Spoiler–Free excerpt from *BAMA 8*

In the distance, the tunnel began to glow softly. Some distance later, the stone hallway opened up, giving way to an enormous cave.

Helesys thoughts drifted back to the flooded caverns of the fishmen and the enormous underground expanses lit by magical torches and littered with rust and ruins.

Here, the torches and fitted stones ended at the hallway, and gave way to jagged, moist rocks. Black rock lined the cavern and rose up hundreds of feet above them, dwarfing even those previous realms. The walls of the cavern were covered in heaping swathes of glowing flowering plants—all manner of deep purples, blues and greens—which cast an eerie glow over the edges of the cavern. The air was humid to the point of haze—not quite to mist—and gave the far walls a surreal underwater glow. The ceiling was so high that the faint lights looked like smudged stars. The cavern seemed to stretch out farther to the sides, as if the area was a massive tunnel.

Helesys and Taunauk stalked silently out from the hall, weapons ready and eyes darting across the glowing landscape, weary of any unseen dangers.

The only movement were ghostly creatures, barely more than a faint white outline and Helesys could scarcely make out more than the faintest of detail. Most walked on all fours and faint outlines of horns and tails could be seen. Others looked Terran and walked on two legs. Of those, Helesys could make out arms and the smallest outline of a hand, but their face and fingers were barely a puff of mist. These ghostly creatures faded in and out of view as if they were made of mist itself, only appearing to stoop at a flower, disappear and reappear at another—as if the flowers somehow gave form to them.

When the creatures did not notice Helesys and Taunauk, the weaver turned her attention to the closest of the glowing flowers. The smallest were nearly two feet across, the largest were wider than she could reach across. Their shapes were alien and absurd—or so Helesys felt—and no two flower shapes or colors seemed to match. Each seemed utterly unique.

"What do you think of this, outlander?" Helesys asked.

Taunauk was studying the flowers similarly. He stowed the Everfall shield and reached into his bag for a small strip of bandage. He wrapped it around his fingers, then rubbed a broadleaf and petal of the nearest flower, then carefully smelled the cloth.

"It does not seem to be poisonous," he said reluctantly. "But give them a wide berth. We've seen too many strange sights to be sure that they are harmless."

To be continued November 2021

Thank you for Reading

I hope you enjoyed reading this story as much as I enjoyed writing it.

If you did, I would massively appreciate a short review on Amazon or your favorite book website. Reviews are crucial for any author, and a starred review or even just a line or two can make a huge difference.

It's especially true for the start of a series. Thanks and I hope you enjoy the next one!

Looking for more Engrossing Fantasy?

You might like ***Tales from Another World,*** an ongoing short story series containing stories about sorcerers, druids, mortals, gods, thieves, and all other manner of Terrans.

The 2nd installment is out and it may or may not have ties to the world of *A Battleaxe and a Metal Arm*. So, if you're looking for more engrossing fantasy stories, read on and see how deep the rabbit hole goes.

What questions do you have about *A Battleaxe and a Metal Arm*?

If you've read this far, hopefully you'll read a bit further—both in this book and across the series. I'm not sure how most authors write serials and how much of it is flying by the seat of their pants, but that's not how I do things. For all the major questions that might come up in BAMA, I already have answers for 95% of them. Same goes for the major plot points, twists and climaxes. That might sound boring to some, especially some of you other authors who enjoy variations of writing into the dark, but I think having a solid blueprint is paramount to writing a long series.

So, what questions do you have about the story? Here are a few:

1) ~~What is the dungeon?~~ It's a soul trap of overwhelming size and power. But where did it come from? Is it a force of nature or an ill-made weapon, or perhaps something else entirely?

2) Who were Helesys and Taunauk before they got trapped? At this point, we know little more than their names and abilities. How well did they know each other beforehand?

3) How did Helesys get her metal arm?

4) Who is Shawn? Why does he feel so familiar to Helesys and Taunauk?

5) Who is the Wolf King and what sinister plans does he have for our heroes? How did he come to rule over the Dungeon? How does the Gatekeeper factor into all this?

6) Who is the mysterious voice encountered on the white sandy shores of Meridian? Why do they seek the death of the Wolf-King? …And why did they choose the heroes?

Did I miss any questions? Probably. Connect with me and other *BAMA* fans on social media and compare questions!

I've got plans. I've got answers. And I've got them on a drip-feed. Keep reading and expect to find out a little more to the mysteries with each installment. Hopefully, you're as excited about this series as I am.

Connect with the Author

If you want to stay up to date on the latest about Samuel's publishing news and blog, check out his website and consider signing up for his monthly newsletter.

www.SamuelFlemingBooks.com

Samuel can also be found on Reddit, Goodreads and Facebook.

Samuel Fleming is a Science Fiction and Fantasy author.

He grew up in Maryland, spending most of his time swimming and writing. Swimming gave him a lot of time to daydream, so the two hobbies complemented each other well. Idle day dreams turned into stories, some of which stuck with him for years. These days he swims a little less and writes a lot more.

He loves a good story no matter the medium: Books, TV, video games, comics, tabletop RPG's, or podcasts–most of which he attempts to share with his wife and three kids, and occasionally on his blog.

www.ingramcontent.com/pod-product-compliance
Lightning Source LLC
Chambersburg PA
CBHW030647190726
48286CB00008B/2701